Home To My Valley

by Paul Green

The University of
North Carolina Press
Chapel Hill

Manufactured in the United States of America
ISBN 0-8078-1148-3
Library of Congress Catalog Card Number 76-123105

For Mildred and Bill

Contents

Introduction

I was born in the Cape Fear River Valley of North Carolina and have spent most of my life there. But over the years it has been necessary now and then, both for financial and artistic reasons, to dwell for quite some time in other parts of the world—whether studying and working in the theatre in Europe, putting on plays in New York, writing motion pictures in Hollywood, or traveling and lecturing in Asia and elsewhere. And two precious years I spent in my youth struggling and doing some fighting in Flanders to make the world safe for democracy. But wherever I have gone, wherever my footsteps have wandered, I have always returned—home to my Valley.

Compared to the wide stretches of the earth's surface this place is not large, being only some two hundred miles long and having an area of less than eight thousand square miles. When one thinks of the deep depressions between mountains elsewhere, this is hardly a valley at all. Its average width is less than forty miles, and the sloping of both its sides toward the river in between is so gentle that a traveler along its now stretching highways would hardly notice it. And the river itself is small, except when it tears loose in rambunctious wildness in freshet times. It is navigable by ships for only forty miles, from Wilmington to the sea, kept open by constant government dredging.

When I was a boy, the gaunt shadow of the Civil War hung like a spectre out of the Apocalypse over this land. Poverty and hardship were the rule. Roads were hardly more than sandbeds then. Hamlets and villages were small and few. Agricultural implements were crude and back-breaking—a crook-handled scythe, a reaper's cradle, a Boy Dixie turn-plow, a middle-buster with ever-loosening steel sweeps and dull point, a guano bugle and wooden bucket, a snaggle-tooth one-man harrow, a heavy hoe, an axe and maul and wedge.

So it was.

I remember on our farm near Buies Creek we would drag the leafless top of a limby oak tree over our fields in winter to cover our sowed-in wheat. Many of the farmers ploughed their land with steers or bull-yearlings in those days, and shallow ploughing it was. Some of the doctors rode horse-back and carried their folk medicines of calomel and blue mass and instruments of diagnosis and often of torture in their saddle-bags. A trip to the town of Dunn fifteen miles from my home was an all-day's journey, but it always had a bright promise waiting at the end of it, even so. For my father and I would get us a good fish dinner at Smith's Cafe for ten cents apiece. And remembering those wonderful dinners now, I still can see and hear the millions of hungry flies that hummed above our heads.

And typhoid fever and cholera-infantum were a curse back then. So were tuberculosis, pneumonia, and malaria. The country schools were small and to be reached in freezing weather over icy footlogs with children sniffling and blowing their noses as they went. And there was always the hard work of the women of the house. Nearly all of the Negro wives cooked in open fireplaces. The white wives were usually better off with wood-burning cook stoves bought from Sears-Roebuck. And there were childbed fever and diphtheria. And the graveyards were populated with babies and young people too-early passed away. And so on the roll call could continue.

Is this a sorrowful listing? Yes. But it is life, life. We were happy. Hope was the same then as now. Love was the same, and birth and death the same. But even so, living was hard, too hard.

Now it is so different. Things have changed in the Valley. The fields are green now even in the freeze of winter and are provided with tractors and all sorts of mechanized implements, resulting in great huge outspilling crops of tobacco, corn, cotton, millet, and soybeans. And gone are the shoulder-galling and salt-caked shirt days of August fodder-pulling. The houses are nicely painted now, and there are electric lights, refrigerators, radio, and television. And good roads are everywhere—leading not only to markets but to huge bright consolidated schools with well-educated teachers and laboratory equipment—and also to fresh churches and community center buildings with their landscaping and flowers and shrubs—and to outdoor dramas and symphony orchestra concerts.

And today the housewives, freed from some of their labor, are holding their book club meetings, their music clubs, their poetry and current events groups. And looking all about, one sees a happy people, healthy, singing, and moving ahead—moving on, whatever the disruptions around, whatever the clamor of the world's distant woes.

And I am back home again now in the latter days of my life. These are not dull and gray days either—no, but rather inspiring and creative ones. For see how the great light breaks over the Valley in the streakings and color-splurgings of the sinking sun. And in that light I now continue my too often interrupted writings about the people I know and love.

So herewith I offer this little volume of stories as a part of that continuing.

P. G.

COTTON CHOPPERS

From *The Frank C. Brown Collection of North Carolina Folklore*, Vol. V, Duke University Press, 1962. Reprinted by permission of the artist, Clare Leighton.

Home To My Valley

Rassie and the Barlow Knife

The barlow is my favorite pocketknife, and I always carry one with me when I can. If I lose it, I quickly try to get another. Back in the early part of the twentieth century they could be bought for twenty-five cents apiece, but I noticed that in the 1970 Sears-Roebuck catalogue they were listed at $2.34 each. My fondness for this most serviceable two-bladed knife goes back to the time when I had a little Negro playmate long, long ago there in Harnett County, by the name of Rassie McLeod.

I remember vividly as if it were yesterday the day Rassie and I, two tiny little boys, first met. I was out in front of my father's house playing in the flat and sand-clogged water ditch. I was small enough to be wearing some sort of a dress then but big enough already to be about my own business which was the making of a frog house. This dirt house was made by burrowing one bare foot in the sand and piling the damp dirt carefully patted and packed over and around and then at the proper time gently pulling the foot out and leaving a snug little cave for any homeseeking frog. Will McLeod, a Negro tenant who had recently moved to my father's farm to live in the one single tenant shack the land afforded, came by. He had a little black boy about my size with him.

"Whatcha doing, fellow?" Will asked me with the genial indulgence Negroes had in those days for small white children.

"Fixing a wog house," I said.

"Now, Lord, ain't that nice. A what?"

"A wog house."

"Whatcha going to put in it?"

"Wogs."

"You mean frogs."

"Wogs."

This seemed to tickle Will, and he laughed and then patted my head when he saw my mother coming across the yard. The little black boy stood there and grinned at me too, and I smiled back.

"Mis' Betty, you ought to hear him talk," Will called out politely as my mother came up with a partly-finished waist-piece in one hand and a pair of scissors in the other. "Yes-suh, talks right up with any the boys," he said.

"I want to try his blouse pattern," my mother said. "Bring him here, Will." Will reached down and pulled me up, and I began yelling and kicking. Mama got down on her knees in front of me, put the cloth piece on my shoulders and pinned it in the back for measurement. I can still remember her pretty pink face and tumbled dark hair. "Now you be quiet," she said. "I'm getting ready to fix you some britches like Rassie's." And I was quiet.

"He and Rassie done sizing up each other's manhood a'ready," Will said. "How old is he, Mis' Betty?"

"He's four this spring, Will."

"Rassie's 'bout four too," said Will. "Can they play together, Mis' Betty?"

"If they don't fight," she said.

When she had finished, she rose, turned, and went back into the house where her other work as always was waiting.

From that day on Rassie and I were cronies. And how free I could run now in my little waist-buttoned trousers Mama soon provided! And most every evening I would beg her and Papa to let me go spend the night at Rassie's house.

"Why, you wouldn't think of going down there, would

you?" my much older half-sister Ellie asked. "I wouldn't want to go and sleep with niggers."

"Rassie ain't no nigger," I said.

"Oh, yes, he is," Ellie said. "Can't you see he's black as sut? And you can smell him too."

But just the same I kept pleading. One day Papa crinkled his eyes toward Mama and said, "Let him go, Betty." And that evening I went joyfully home with Rassie. Will's Zella, a big bosomed, smoky-eyed woman, as I remember her, had supper already on a table lighted by a flickering lamp, and her three sons were all lined up waiting around it. The oldest was Herbert, the next Preacher, and then Rassie. And when she put me and all of the little fellows on benches around the table and poured out some black sorghum molasses and gave us each a piece of ragged cornbread, I thought it was nice and fine, everybody seemed to be feeling so good. But still I wasn't hungry. Three pairs of skinny black hands grabbed the bread and sopped it into the molasses and the Negro boys ate greedily away. But I didn't eat. In the dusky darkness that filled the room a million flies it seemed were humming about and swarming above our heads, and a queer smell was in the air. In our house there were lots of flies too, but not that smell. A lump kept rising up and sticking in my throat, and all of a sudden I knew I was going to cry. My big bragging and boasting to my papa and mama about how I would like to live in Rassie's house always was now clear forgot.

"Why don't he eat?" Will said. "Help him, Zella." And Zella broke off a piece of bread, dipped it into the molasses and stuck it into my mouth. I choked and blubbered, and a shower of crumbs blew out over the table. Herbert and Preacher and Rassie all giggled together, but Rassie was silent first.

"I don't want nothing," I mumbled, and a flood of hot tears gushed to my eyes as I began to cry with hog-wild grief.

“Huh,” said Zella, “I know, he wants his mammy.” The two older brothers looked at me in wide astonishment, and Rassie came over and put his arms around me. I hugged him tight, sniveling and sputtering with sobs.

The next thing I remember was the lonely dark road and Will walking back up the sandbed with me, holding me by the hand, and now and then when the sand was too deep, lifting and carrying me in his arms.

For many a day after that my older sister Ellie teased me about being a ’fraidy-cat and a crybaby, and I was so burnt up with shame at first that I went off behind the barn where the hired fodder hands did their business and wiped themselves with corncobs, and I leant my face against the cold boards there in the stink and wept bitterly, feeling too that Rassie might be ashamed of me. But he wasn’t, as I found out next day when he came to play.

He and I were too small to plow or do much hoeing in the fields for the next two or three years, though in the fall we would pick cotton with the rest of the folks. And through the long summertimes we went exploring in the swamps and wading in the cool sluggish creek, looking for pikes and jacks and other fish that might be lying still and asleep in the shallow sunny water. We made ourselves a couple of bows out of small split hickory saplings and arrows and gigs out of umbrella ribs to spear fish there in the deep swamp. We went hunting for birds too, wandering hours and hours in the woods with beanshooters made out of strips of old bicycle inner tubes. We got so we could knock a sapsucker off a limb same as a man with a rifle—or so we said we could. And we made rabbit-boxes and set them in the fence jambs where the gnawings on the bottom rails showed that Br’er Rabbit was used to travel. But for some reason we were never able to catch any rabbits.

In confidential discussion our schemes grew vast and manifold for selling furs and making ourselves rich with silver and gold. We had already figured it out that in the fall we would pick enough cotton for hire at twenty-five cents a hundred to buy steel traps. These we'd set along the creek where the otters had their slide and the muskrats their home. Two dollars a hide that man over in Lillington had said he would pay for them on delivery. Rassie was especially anxious to make some money so we could buy a whole box of Apple chewing tobacco. But we never got any steel traps or made any money from furs. Still we got a bit of tobacco now and then. I found where Papa kept his plugs of chewing in the tray compartment of his old trunk and I used to slip in there with a butcher knife or scissors and peel off little thin slices across the ends which he never would notice, and I always gave Rassie his share.

And Rassie taught me many things—taught me how to pop my finger joints, how to spit tobacco juice through my front teeth, how to put my two fingers in my mouth and give a keen and ear-tingling whistle, how to put my cupped hand under my arm and with pumpings of my crooked elbow make vulgar breaking-wind sounds that tickled us both into gales of giggles—taught me too how to bandage up sores with Jimson weeds and chew sassafras bark or green pine needles to kill off the power of nicotine and the smell of chewing tobacco on our breath. He taught me also how to put peas up my nose and snort them out like dogwood berries from a popgun.

Then he told me that if we would get a fish-swimmer out of a little fish and I would swallow it, I would then be able to swim like that fish. So with a hook baited with a flat-head worm out of a rotten log we finally caught a little pike, cut him open, took out the inflated tiny air sac, and with great swallows of creek water I finally got the sac down. Then to Rassie's prompting I took off my clothes and dived into the creek. But I sank to the bottom like a rock, and Rassie had to jump in, clothes and all, and pull me out—laughing and whooping and confessing then that he'd been tricking me the way old man Cofield had once tricked him.

I was mad as hops for a while, but I soon forgave my partner, for in the next few weeks he showed me really how to swim—and how to tread water and float on my back like a cork too.

Rassie knew all kinds of games, like driving imaginary horses with strips of mulberry bark for reins the while he gave his loud commands of gee and haw, and yoking little pigs for fun. We would go down into Papa's hog pasture and catch a baby pig and put a small forked limb we'd trimmed with Rassie's barlow knife around its neck, tie it with a string, and then we would watch the pig run and turn somersaults when the tongue of the yoke caught in the earth. And we would roll on the ground ourselves in fun.

One day I received a surprise. When I thought about it later I knew I shouldn't have been surprised, but at the time I was. Rassie was trimming a dogwood sprout fork to make a beanshooter staff, when his knife slipped and he nicked his finger. It bled a bit.

"Look-a there at that!" I said.

"Look-a there at what?" said Rassie unconcernedly as he wrapped a green oak leaf around his finger and went on scraping and notching the staff.

"At—at your blood—you bleed like that," I said.

"Lawd, just a scratch," said Rassie. "It didn't hurt none, and I ain't no whiny-baby. It's 'bleeged to bleed some."

"I mean it's red—red same like me when I have the nose-bleed."

Rassie stared at me a moment. I can still see him wrinkling his nose. "Co'sen it's red," he said. And then he spoke up a little sharply, "You figure it'd be differenter?"

"I 'spected maybe—I don't know," I answered, a little shamefaced now before my partner's searching look.

Rassie let out his little dog-yelping laugh. "Mebbe 'cause I'm black you was thinking my blood would be black. Go 'way from here, boy! Where you got your brains—in your setter?"

And I said I was glad his blood was the same color as mine. And after that I felt closer to my friend than ever.

And the days were swift and golden then, and I loved my little black playmate better than father or mother or anybody else in the whole wide world and I planned that we would stay together always.

Then came the end of that year and bitter separation. Will's crop had turned out poorly, and he and his family moved over to Mr. Darius Hodges's place, a landlord a few miles away. But in the third year the McLeods were back in their little shack on Papa's land, there to remain for several years now that a lull seemed to have come in both their tenant farm curiosity and their hopes. And my and Rassie's friendship was fervently renewed.

That was a terrible summer around the neighborhood the year he and I were ten. At the supper table I would hear Papa and Mama speak about old Mrs. Morgan or Mr. Jones's family or somebody being sick with the fever. The scourge had spread up and down among the tenant farmers along the Cape Fear River swamps like cholera among hogs. The people kept dying, the hammer kept ringing, and most of the dried boards in the farmers' sheds had been used for coffins. One day in the road near our house I heard Dr. Joe McKay speaking to Papa about flies and filth causing the typhoid fever to be so bad.

"You ought to screen that tenant house of yours down there, Billy," the doctor said. And Papa replied that once he had screened the house and the lowdown tenants had knocked the screens out and kept on answering the call of nature beside the well curb or off the edge of the porch wherever and whenever the need struck them.

"I've grown up with tenants, worked with 'em, lived with 'em, and you can't change 'em," he said firmly.

I knew he was talking about Rassie's people and my face burnt with shame. And then Doctor Joe said maybe Papa was right at that and after all no man need hope to live long enough to teach these niggers any sense, but anyway he thought he'd speak about it.

And the angel of death kept going up and down the land knocking on people's doors. But he never knocked at our door. Maybe it was because my mama who was an up-and-coming woman, as all the neighbors said, had long ago seen to it that we had a nice garden house at the back with lime and ashes sprinkled in it and there were screens on the windows and doors of our house.

But finally this dread summons came to Will McLeod's family. The first to fall sick was Herbert, the oldest son, and then the second son, Preacher, was taken down. Papa was run ragged with all this sickness and grassy crops around, and I heard him telling my older half-sister Ellie that she would have to go down to Will's house and see what she could do. He had to mow his crowfoot grass hay in the bottom and besides that he had to see about getting his late nitrate of soda and top-dressing stuff brought from the railroad siding—a world of things to do. And as for Mama, she was all big and swollen now with the new baby we all knew would soon be coming and had to stay quiet. So Ellie got her sunbonnet and went off across the field. I followed her.

"Is Rassie sick?" I asked anxiously.

"Not that I know of," said Ellie.

"I'm going down there to see," I said.

"No, I reckon you won't," she answered. "You've got to keep out of this business." But I followed her on by the mulberry orchard, and when I didn't go back, she picked up a stick and chased me off same as if I had been a little dog.

The next morning when I went in to eat my breakfast, there Ellie sat all tired and hollow-eyed.

"Rassie's sick, too," she was saying to Papa and Mama, "and Will and Zella are on the puny list and not a bit of good."

"Is he bad?" I whispered.

"Yes, it's bad!" she almost shouted.

"That's the way it is," said Mama, "when the fever strikes, it usually has to run through the whole family."

And Papa sat there blowing on the hot coffee in his saucer to cool it and staring through the door toward the open field.

"It's hard on Will," he said, "hard on us all. I just heard that Mis' Delaney Morgan died last night. Aye, the Lord giveth, and the Lord taketh away." And he got up as if stung by some irritating and frustrating thought and strode out of the house.

"I got to go down there again," Ellie said, pulling herself up out of her chair. "It's bad, I tell you."

"I'm going with you this time, Ellie," I said stoutly as she passed out onto the porch.

"No, you ain't. The doctor don't want nobody messing around there, only I've got to go." And Mama spoke up too and said for me to stay at home.

The next day when I took the water jug down in the field for Papa and his new hired hand, I slipped off by a hedge and prayed a little prayer for Rassie, and I cried a little bit. And after that I felt good and knew that Rassie must already be better. It seemed like the Lord had answered me to say so. I would slip down across the pasture there to Will's house and see. When I came by the log crib I saw one of the pigs sleeping there in the sun. He was lying on his side and had on a yoke Rassie and I had tied on him a few days before. Rassie had stumped his big toe bad and torn the nail trying to catch that very pig.

When I got in the edge of the yard, I heard a low moaning and wailing going on in the house that chilled the heart in me and shortened my steps in two. I had heard that kind of racket before at some of the buryings in Pleasant Plains churchyard. Yes, something was wrong, bad wrong. Doctor Joe was there too, his buggy-horse hitched to a swinging limb before the little shack of a house. And then I heard

Will's loud voice calling out like a mourner at a funeral service—

> He's done gone, gone,
> Done passed over the icy water!

And creeping shiveringly up by the stick-and-dirt chimney, I looked in through the window. There Will and Zella were squatted on the floor weaving their heads back and forth and flinging up their hands, then lowering their heads again with bumps against the planking and pouring out a roll of disjointed prayers and moaning sounds. Ellie came out on the porch and stared at me.

"You better go right on back home," she ordered.

"How is he?" I asked. "How is he?"

"Nohow," she answered in the same tired hopeless way, turning back into the house.

I crept up on the porch and looked in at the door. How clear it all comes back to me now. Over in the corner was a homemade plank bed, and Doctor Joe was standing by it with his watch in his hand. Among the tangle of dirty quilts lay two moaning shuddering black creatures with rolling delirious eyes, and in their poor faces, peaked and thin from their great suffering and fever-burning, I recognized Herbert and Preacher. Herbert was making low guttural sounds in his throat and smacking his feverish lips, and out of Preacher's mouth a flock of awful noises was pouring, gurgles and chokings like a half-strangled suckling pig. But I wasn't looking at him now. My eyes kept searching around the shadow-filled room for Rassie.

Ellie came in from the lean-to kitchen at the back with a cloth and a pan and a big cake of homemade soap in her hand. She went across to the far corner of the room and knelt down, and then I saw Rassie lying there on a pallet by the hearth with a piece of Zella's old bright-patterned skirt thrown over him and his head resting on a little bed-ticking pillow stuffed with straw. He was asleep.

"Rassie, Rassie!" Will moaned.

"Rassie, Rassie!" Zella shrieked in wild lament.

And I began shaking as if with a chill, shaking like old Miss Minty Gaskins with the palsy. No, no, it couldn't be that. Rassie was asleep; he was resting now. Ellie set the pan of water down, dipped the cloth in it, and held the wet wad padded in her hand as if waiting for something.

Then Doctor Joe snapped the lid of his big gold watch to with a sound like the bite of a steel trap, or so the sound seemed to me. And he picked up his little black bag and started out of the room.

"Yeh, let him stay if he wants to," he said, glaring red-eyed down at me, "Let him stay! Let 'em all stay—and die!"

Turning around in the room as if blind with anger, he spoke above the bed on which the two boys lay. "Look-a there, will you, stink-hole of filth! Why in the name of God a good man like Billy Green allows his tenants to live so—ah!" And he threw up his free hand, baffled and despairing. Then jamming on his big white panama hat, he stamped out of the house, calling back to Ellie as he clomped down the rickety porch, "I'll come again tomorrow or the next day. It don't do no good, but I'll come. You got some medicine there. Give it to 'em."

And Ellie kept dipping the cloth into the water and wadding it in her hand. Now she suddenly whipped off the old skirt that covered Rassie and showed him lying there helpless and cold in death.

"Rassie, Rassie!" I screamed.

"Shut your mouth," Ellie muttered.

Rassie's little thin legs were stuck out straight as two pencils from a stomach stretched and bloated like a watermelon or a rubber balloon you get at a circus. And purging, oozing stuff was coming out of his mouth. Will and Zella kept moaning and beating their fists and foreheads on the floor and crying out, "God done took him! God done took him away!" And all the while, like a limb scraping against the shingles of a house, the shucking, blubbering sound from Preacher's throat kept rising and falling in the room.

And now Ellie began to bathe Rassie's forehead and then the top of his head, kinky wool and all. I dropped down on my knees and held out my hand. With a look out of her tired hollow eyes, she unfolded the cloth, tore it in two, and handed me a piece. Dipping the rags into the pan and wringing them out again, the two of us washed the little dark body and made it ready for the grave.

"What caused him to swell up like that?" I whispered, and even above the moans of Will and Zella, Ellie heard me.

"Gas, the doctor said."

"When did it happen?" I mumbled. And I didn't wait to hear what she said, for now I had to wipe that purging stuff again that kept seeping out from Rassie's lips.

"This morning about day," she said. Then she got up and told me to finish, and I knew she was ashamed to wash between Rassie's legs and all. And so I did as softly and gently as I could. But when I got to Rassie's sore toe with its torn nail, I let that be, for I didn't want to hurt him so. Finally when I was through, I sat back on my haunches and looked at my dead comrade, and I still remember the trickles of hot tears that kept running down on either side of my nose and dropping between my feet to the floor.

Ellie came back and knelt down again, unrolled a paper parcel and took out a clean white sleeping-shirt.

"I don't reckon you'll mind," she said, shaking it out and running it back over her bent arm. I saw that it was my own nightshirt, the one I bought cloth for a few weeks before with my quarter I'd earned from helping Mis' Tew clean the nutgrass out of her vegetable garden.

"I'm glad for him to have it," I said.

"Help me," she gestured.

We lifted Rassie's scrawny shoulders, and I later remembered—though I didn't think of it then—how pitifully cold he was to my touch, and we slipped the shirt over him, straightened him out, and laid him back still and peaceful on his quilt.

Ellie now took a knife from the mantelpiece and handed it to me. It was Rassie's barlow, the one we'd used so much in cutting the yokes for the pigs and carving our little pine-bark ships and little water-wheel whirligigs when the freshets were on in the ditches and field furrows.

"This morning before day he reared up from his pallet and, pointing over there, said to give it to you. I reckon it's a fair swap," she went on in her tired voice, "he gets the shirt and you the knife, and they fit the needs of both of you. Now go home and tell Pa somebody's got to fix him a coffin. Will and Zella ain't worth a cent to help."

That afternoon Papa and I sawed boards and made a wooden box for Rassie. And I got a roll of cotton from a bale in the yard and put it as a soft pillow for his head.

Then we carried the box down to Will's house and laid Rassie gently in it. And when he was fixed and easy there, we took the hammer and nails and fastened down the lid over him. And Will said, "Bury him anywhere, Mr. Billy, anywhere you will. Maybe up there in the field by the cedar tree. I ain't got no heart to help."

It was evening now and almost dark, but I got an old shovel from the little crib, and we went up into the fields and there under the big cedar tree we dug Rassie's grave and buried him. And when we were ready to go, I said, "Ain't you going to say a little something over him, Papa?" My father hesitated a moment, pulled off his hat, and then murmured out a few words in the thickening gloom, "In such an hour as ye know not the Son of Man cometh and we all got to be ready to go at the last day, blessed be his Holy Name." But he said nothing about Rassie's being in Heaven, for like a great many folks in North Carolina at that time he was still a bit uncertain as to whether Negroes really had full-fledged souls and would be allowed in Heaven. But I knew that Rassie had gone straight to

Heaven and was right at that moment standing close by the throne of God and was being petted and taken care of by the lovely angels gathered round. And when Papa went on home ahead of me, calling back for me to come on, I drove a sharp little piece of plank down for a headboard. It was good dark now and the evening star was shining close by the frail upturned moon low in the west. I took out the barlow knife and in the gloom carved as best I could a rough cross on the plank. Next day when it was good daylight I would come and cut some words—"Rassie—he sleeps here"—to his memory, real words, yes.

"I'll do it, Rassie," I said aloud. "I'll do it. Rest, Rassie, rest right good," I said.

A long while I stood there, looking down at the grave, the hot tears again scalding my face. Then with swelling, breaking heart I turned and, clutching my precious knife tight in my hand, followed after my father.

June Sweet'nings

"Speaking of June Sweet'nings," Uncle Myron Lassiter said to me one day, "reminds me of old Guy Fitchett and his wife Bessie. They lived down the road a piece from where my daddy's house was then, there where the highway turns from Corinth toward old Haywood. The house has been torn down long ago and the apple orchard with it to make room for progress on the highway. I believe there's still one scraggly old tree, though, a sort of stump near the road that sprouts out now and then. I noticed it the last time I went down to Brickhaven. The Fitchetts were mighty proud of that apple orchard. And me and my sister Josie loved to eat them June Sweet'nings, better'n anything in the world. My sister was older'n me and she was quick-legged. One day old Guy found us up in one of his apple trees there gathering and guzzling some and he switched us out of there and told us to behave ourselves and never bother his apples again—or else. Well, my sister Josie was a quick-tempered little old thing and she didn't forget the switching. No sir, nor the threat.

"Well, I told you a while ago about the steamboat, *The Haughton*, that old man Brady run up the Cape Fear River. He quit running it after the railroads come in. And after some of the locks were washed out in the big freshet, he anchored it in the Cape Fear not far from our house—it stayed there year after year, rotting away.

"One day I was down there, a little barefooted boy proguing around, when I found something lying across the deck about eight feet long, looked like a long black snake. I'd never seen one of these hose pieces before. So I got it loose from its fastening and broke it off, with a little sharp piece of iron at the end of it, and I drug it up the hill to take it home. I met my sister Josie. 'What is that?' she said.

" 'I dunno,' I said. 'I found it down there on the old steamboat rotting away.'

"She looked at it for a while and then she said, 'I got a use for that.'

" 'What use you got?' I said.

" 'I got a use,' she said. 'Will you give it to me?'

"So I let her have it. I didn't know what it was anyhow. That youngun, that sister of mine, she really had a mind. She'd already seen some possibilities in that thing that looked like a snake. No wonder she later married a man who is a professor up there at Chapel Hill and has raised a lot of educated boys and girls of her own.

"Finally she told me what she was planning. She was determined to scare old man Fitchett out of his wits. So we cooked up a thing, she done the cooking of course, since I was a little shaver two years younger. She was about twelve years old or thirteen and I was about nine or ten, and I looked up to her in her smartness and wisdom.

"So we went up toward the Fitchett house and lay around out in the edge of the woods there till we saw old man Fitchett and his wife go down to the barn to milk the cow and tend to things. So we crope into the house there the back way and found their bed. We pulled the cover down and put that thing down at the foot of the bed, quiled it around and stuck its head up, and then put the sheet back and the quilt across it so nobody could tell what was what.

"Well that night after we'd gone home and got our supper Josie said we'd go back and call on the Fitchetts, so we did, and we sat around and we talked and we kept 'em up quite a while. And Josie got to asking about stories, about snake stories and ghost stories. And old Guy, he was a skerry fellow anyhow and his wife, Mis' Bessie, weren't much better. So long about midnight he up and said, 'Why don't you children go on home and quit talking these wild stories?'

"And so we said we were just about to go. We told 'em goodnight. 'And don't you let the boogers get you,' Mis' Bessie said, all sharplike, 'going home.'

" 'Oh, we won't,' said Josie, 'We won't. We ain't scared of anything except snakes. And you and Mr. Guy watch out for snakes, too!'

" 'Go on,' said old man Fitchett.

" 'They do tell some of 'em are fearful things,' said Josie. 'My grandpa Avery down at White Oaks got followed by a coachwhup snake once. It rolled down a hill right after him and he nearly run hisself to death. I just remember the story now. He dodged behind a tree and that hoopsnake made for him and soused the p'int of its tail up in the tree behind which Grandpa had dodged!

"I had a hard time to keep from laughing, for she was telling a story we'd both heard happened to a man way off in Georgy or somewhere.

" 'And you know,' she went on, 'the next day that tree had all its leaves quiled up and it died plumb dead.'

" 'We ain't scared of snakes,' said Mis' Bessie. But she was—yessir, scared to death of 'em. And so we went off. We watched them turn back in the house and shut the door, and then we crope back and stood behind a spirea bush outside the window where there were big windowpanes that we could see through. So we stayed outside and watched 'em.

"Purty soon old man Guy took off his clothes and stood naked as a jaybird and my sister of course had to turn away her head at that. And then he put on his long red nightshirt and knitted toque, and I pinched Josie and told her she could look now. And then we watched him go down on his knees and say his prayers. He was a mighty religious old fellow and was superstitious too. And while he was a-prayin' Mis' Bessie put on her nightgown and undressed herself under it, and I was glad she did, for I didn't want to see her naked, skinny and old as she was. Well, old man Guy he got up and pulled back the cover a little and got in the bed and slid down in it. And then we saw him all of a sudden freeze up, his hands lifting like calling for help and his feet and knees all drawed up. And he lay there shivering and shaking, not saying a word. Truth is he was scared speechless and couldn't speak, I reckon. Mis' Bessie finished saying her prayers and started to get in the bed. And she saw him lying there, his face blue as a huckleberry, and choking like a man strangling to death.

" 'What is it, what is it, Sweetum?' she said. She loved him so she always called him 'Sweetum.'

"Finally the breath blew from him in a great gust and he

got some words out. 'Snakes!' he yelled, 'snakes, I fully believe!' And with that he sailed out of that bed, jerking the cover off. And there lay that black thing all quiled up in the dim lamplight, looking like a snake sure enough with its head stuck up. Well sir, old man Fitchett had a heavy walking stick with a piece of iron on it. He used it when he walked about to be sure to keep any bothersome dogs off of him. He was always scared of mad dogs. So he had fixed up this walking stick special heavylike. Mis' Bessie grabbed that walking stick out of his hand, and while Josie and me stood outside just popping with laughing, she sailed onto the snake with that stick. And she beat and tore into the featherbed to a fare you well. They had two ticks together, all stuffed with feathers. But she busted 'em both. She busted the pillows, too, and in no time the room was so full of feathers you couldn't see a thing. What happened in the turmoil and turning was that not being able to see a thing, in one of her heavy strokes at the snake she laid old man Guy Fitchett right across the side of the head with that iron stick and plumb addled him. Yes, sir, later the doctor had to come and sew up his skelp with fourteen stitches, so he did.

"Well, as you might 'spect, somehow the Fitchetts got on to who done that tricking. They found out that Josie and me were to blame, and they come down to my house and told my daddy, and he said, 'All right, Josie!' and he reached for the razor strop.

"So they marched us both up there. And old Mis' Fitchett she give us them cards—you know them things with the fine teeth which you card cotton wool with or used to. Well she give Josephine one of 'em and give me the other and put us to cleaning that room. Them feathers had stuck to the rafters and the weatherboard in a thick coating of white—it was rough weatherboarding—and it took us three solid days to get that stuff off of there. And Mis' Fitchett stood around with that stick guarding things and seeing that we cleaned everything well. Old Guy's skelp had been sewed up by this time and he was lying up in another room with a hot bag of salt to his temple, and so was unable to take part in the proceedings.

"Poor old man Fitchett—he wore a scar long as he lived. Josie and me cried a lot about his scar, but it done no good, none of course."

The Age of Accountability

The first time I ever ran into this accountability matter was when I was a little boy about eleven years old. It was such a hellish experience that the details of it are with me to this day.

The August summer morning was beautiful and fresh, and I was on my way up the road from our farmhouse with a milk bucket swinging in my hand. I was going to the mulberry orchard pasture some two hundred yards off where Liza the cow was waiting to be milked. My heart was happy that morning. The sun was just rising in the east, and the spotted dappled cloudlets were flying across its smiling kindly face, presaging rich rain to come on the greedy crops. The air was warm and scented and tickled the back of my neck and my cheeks sweetly as it scudded across the wide dew-dripping corn and cotton fields. Suddenly I heard a man's heavy voice calling from the direction of our house—a voice that shocked me and sent a crawling depressed feeling along my shoulders and down my backbone.

"Hey!" called the voice. I stopped still as a post. It was Mr. Wicker, the preacher, calling. A big meeting was going on in the neighborhood at the time, and he had spent the night with us as was the custom around and about among the neighbors during a "protracted meeting" of those days. These big or protracted meetings, or revivals, were customary throughout the countryside during the "laying by time," that is, during the period when the final plowing, chopping, siding, and cleaning out the crops had been finished and a waiting of some two or three weeks ensued. Then would begin the burning, blazing business of fodder-pulling, and after that the cotton picking, and then the corn gathering, the corn shucking, the school days coming on and finally the rich fat wintertime to follow. (Back in those days tobacco—a full crowded summer crop—had not taken over in the Valley as it has now.)

I didn't need to turn around to see the preacher. I could visualize his long lanky form and his big drooping yellow mustache coming up behind me. In a moment he stood beside me.

"Mind if I go along with you, Brother Paul?" he said.

"Nuh—no, sir," I stammered.

We went on together.

"I want to talk with you, Brother Paul," he said.

"Yeh—yes, sir," I said.

"You have reached the age of accountability, haven't you, Brother Paul?"

"I—I—don't know, sir," I stammered.

"You are past ten years old, your mother tells me, and are now able to tell right from wrong, ain't you? Sure, you must be."

"I—I—reckon so," I mumbled. I was so embarrassed and

hacked that my one hand free from the milking bucket fluttered about in the air. I stooped and picked up a loose little rock here and there and sent it sailing through the air to help take the pressure off.

"Sure and most certainly you do," Mr. Wicker continued, "for ten years is the age when you reach the line, and you're beyond that."

He had a way of writhing his hands together, especially when he was down on his knees in the pulpit and invoking God's help and mercy on "us pore needy creatures." And now his hands were writhing together in the old accustomed way. Maybe he was embarrassed too, but so deep was my distress and confusion that I didn't think of him being in like condition. The truth is he was a terrible and mighty power walking along in the sandbed with me and the awe-ful voice of God was in his voice.

"It's time to give your little heart to Jesus," he said strongly, even sternly, "don't you think so?"

"Yes sir, yes sir—I reckon so."

A sparrow singing away was sitting in a wild peach tree in the fence jamb, and I sailed a rock at the little bird. And blam! I hit him smack, and he tumbled to the ground. The preacher stopped and looked at me. I stopped too.

"I believe you killed him," he said, "that bird."

"Maybe so, sir," I said, my heart suddenly heavy in me and yet elated too that I had been so dexterous in my throwing. We went on up the road.

"Now when we get to the church today," he continued, "and I send out the call for sinners to come on to the anxious bench, that blessed seat of salvation and grace, I want you to come down the aisle and kneel there and pray for forgiveness." Suddenly he bellowed and his voice shook me to my toes. "And forgiveness will come! Amen! Hallelujah, praise God's holy name!" I shivered and picked up another small stone as we walked on.

"Will you do that for me?" he said fervently. "Do it for your little soul's sake, my son."

"Yes sir, yes sir, I will do it," I gulped, not daring to say no to this almighty presence walking by me now, overshadowing me, yes, and darkening the whole sky for me now.

I came to the barn lot gate and hoped he would leave me in peace there, but he went on through with me.

"Whilst you're milking I'll stay and talk with you awhile," he said. "Sister Betty tells me she named you for 'Postle Paul, and she plans for you to be a preacher."

I had already developed some definite hidden-away ideas of my own about being a preacher and going up and down the earth spouting God's wrath on such poor helpless human beings as myself the way Brother Goff and Brother Rolland did there at old Pleasant Union Church and the way Mr. Wicker was spouting it on me now.

"She tells me you have already read the Bible through onct."

"Yes sir," I confessed, my face burning with a mixture of shame, pride, and dismay.

"Good, very good," he said, "and our Father in Heaven looks down on you and is pleased at what you are doing. He is, Brother Paul."

A redheaded sapsucker was pecking merrily away on a mulberry limb ahead of us. Not thinking, I let fly the stone I carried, and blam! again, I hit that bird. He tumbled to the ground, fluttered bumpingly about, finally straightened up on his feet and wing tips and flew wobbling away. Mr. Wicker jumped back, put his hands on his hips and from his great height looked down on me. For a moment he said nothing. Finally he spoke up in a queer sharp voice. "What kind of a witness have we here? Do, Lord, tell."

"Sir?" I murmured.

"Do you do that often—knock birds out of trees like that? Why, fellow, you're same as a shotgun, and this time you throwed with your left hand."

Some two years before this a bad bone disease had seized me in my right arm, which had required an operation at Johns Hopkins Hospital to heal me, and during the long period I had learned to throw with my left hand.

"Go ahead and tell me," he said, "first you throw with your right hand and then with your left, and both times you hit the bird. How do you do that?"

"I don't know, sir. I just did." And I knew then that if I had intended to hit those birds, I couldn't have done it. It was "just one of those things."

"Yes, indeedy," the preacher hurried on. "You're a remarkable fellow, I can see that, and if you become a preacher and can hit sinners with the word of God the way you hit them birds with them rocks, why, Dwight L. Moody and Ira D. Sankey and Billy Sunday hisself won't be in it. Yes sir, son, it's the truth. And I misdoubt not that this very morning your doing that to them birds was a sign sent to me from God on high that this is so." And he raised his eyes sanctimoniously and confidingly aloft. "So remember now," he continued, "when I give the call this morning, you are coming down to the front to find Jesus and Him crucified. You promise."

"Yes sir, yes sir," I murmured haltingly.

"Praise God from whom all blessings flow!" he shouted again, his voice echoing across the fields and his hands writhing themselves together as before. Turning, he plunged through the gate, slamming it behind him, and the vibration of his power and speed stopped me where I stood and seemed to shake the earth as well. I stumbled toward the patient waiting cow. I fed her, and as I squatted pulling away at her fat yellow tits, my head buried against her warm friendly flank, I began to cry, and the tears dropped into the milk bucket with the milk, but little did I care. Ahead of me waited the dreadful day at the church. And deep within me was a vast and mighty curse, however wordless, that there ever had been such a thing as the age of accountability and that I had reached it.

Somehow I lasted through the sermon that day, and the singing that followed. Then when the call came I managed to go down the aisle and kneel barefooted at the anxious bench along with older and more sinful creatures such as Eddie Kirk Maxton, who fired the boiler at a neighbor's sawmill and who could never get up steam except to a loud hollering and rolling of profanity. He was yelling to God now, pleading with him to save him from the burning pit, there where the devil waited with his red-hot pitchfork to spear him and jab him down in the melted running brimstone floods of hell. The soles of my bare feet were turned toward the congregation, and my tears were wetting my fingers spread over my face. Then Brother Wicker came and knelt beside me and his bad breath from his decaying teeth blew in on me. He thumped me on the back with the flat of his mighty hand. "Give it up! Give it up!" he shouted. "Let Jesus into your heart! Let Him in! He will save you, save you now! Pray for grace! Pray!" And with a final and devastating blow on my poor little scrawny shoulders, he moved over to belabor Eddie Kirk.

I prayed for grace as he ordered but could feel no grace. The consciousness of my bare feet bothered me, and then my blouse—the one my mother had made with lace around the collar—kept sliding up above my cloth belt, leaving my back bare, and I could feel the fishhooking eyes of a hundred people digging into my naked skin. Even then I might have got some grace if a certain incident hadn't happened. The preacher had moved from the loud clamoring Eddie over to my cousin, Malcolm Norris, who was a notorious sinner, especially with young women, and had already sired a lusty bastard baby boy on confiding and gentle Sally O'Brien and who had been finally persuaded by Miss Myrtle Merritt, another sweet Christian girl who loved him to distraction, to come forward and seek his Savior.

Malcolm was bent there by the open side door of the church. Mr. Wicker knelt by him and began to work on him and with him—and as it turned out, to work in vain.

Now in this neighborhood lived a carpenter named Morgan Ennis. Morgan would never go into the church but always stood outside in his overalls in warm weather to listen to the sermon. In winter he rarely attended service. He always carried a foot ruler in his leg pocket too. Mr. Wicker had a tremendously large foot, and while I was there pleading with some invisible Power to send forth His salvation and provide me happiness hereafter and safety from that awful fire in which sinners broiled in flames seven times hotter than any that burnt on earth and where the devil and his imps dipped molten red-running iron for cool ice cream, I saw Morgan stealthily pull out his foot ruler, lean inside the door, and measure the preacher's huge foot. Later he said it was seventeen inches long.

The thing tickled me so that I forgot where I was and began to snicker. And the preacher and others surely thought it was the holy giggles or happy weepings that had seized upon me—a condition that often did take those in an especially joyous condition of salvation following forgiveness of sin. And old Miss Katie Mitchell who had worked for my mother in times past and who had taken a sort of fancy to me, I thought, now jumped up in hysterics and began to shout, "Glory to God and all the angels on high, my boy is saved! Saved!" And the congregation loudly amen-ed her that this was a fact.

Later when Mr. Wicker called for all the new converts to stand together before the pulpit and receive the right hand of fellowship, I was lined up right there straight among them, and I knew I was a low-down hypocrite and no more saved than a snake had hips. But I would commit most any kind of sin, I knew too, to escape a repetition of that dreadful preceding experience.

So it was that I was "saved from nature to grace" and

three weeks later was baptized with the others in the Reuben Matthews millpond. And since that time I have bothered no more about the age of accountability.

Izzy Izzard and the Crows

Nearly every time I see a crow or think of one I think of Izzy Izzard. His name actually was Israel, Israel Izzard. The Izzards lived between Elizabethtown and Wilmington close by the river, and Norman Izzard, the father, was mainly a corn farmer. Every spring he was mightily tormented by the crows pulling up his young sprouting corn. Like the other farmers he put up scare-crows with their sprawled and motionless gesticulation in the field, and as always the crows got onto the sham and came in the early daybreak to go after the sprouting corn as hard as ever. Izzy the son was about fifteen the year Norman was laying out plans for his biggest corn crop. During the winter he and the hands had got in several more acres of new ground and he was counting on his biggest acreage.

"We ought to make the best crop we've ever made," he said, "if the dang crows will but let us alone."

Now Izzy had already shown a sharpness for making a trade here and there and he had quite a bit of small change saved up in a tin can in his bureau drawer. For instance, when Norman would take the children, say, on an excursion to Wilmington and give each of them two dollars to spend, Izzy would bring most of his back to go into the tin can. He would look a lot and buy little. And another thing that showed his saving and already stingy nature was the way he got his pencils at school. He'd find a student who had a new lead pencil and would say to him, "I'll let you break that there pencil over my head if you'll let me have the piece that falls." And then often crack, crack would go the pencil until it was broken in two. But Izzy never flinched, and he always had a piece of pencil to write with that didn't cost him a penny. So he up and says to his father, "About the crows. What would you give, Pa, for each dead crow?"

"Plenty," said his daddy, "but you can't shoot a crow. They're too smart. You know that, for we've been down there in the field many a time before light waiting for 'em and they didn't come. They knew we were there. And when you try to creep up on 'em, the watchman crow they always have sitting off in a high tree gives the alarm and off they go—caw, caw. No, they ain't no getting by a crow."

"Looks like a crow hadn't ort to be smarter than human folks," said Izzy.

"Yeh, but they are," said his daddy, "smarter about not letting you kill 'em."

"But how much would you give if somebody could kill 'em, Pa?" asked Izzy.

"I'd give a whole silver quarter apiece for 'em," he said, "and I mean it."

"Shake hands on it, Pa," said Izzy.

"Sure thing," said his pa. And they did. Then his daddy went on, "I know you've got a good head on your shoulders for a boy, Izzy," he said, "and just the other day your Uncle Tom said to me after he'd paid you for shearing his kicking mule's tail that no doubt someday you'd be a rich man."

"That'd be fine," said Izzy, all pleased.

"Yeh, he said that. And if you're smart enough to kill any of them crows I'll believe him."

"I'll see what I can do," said Izzy.

Sometime before this Izzy had heard an old wild-turkey hunter say that the way to kill turkeys was to bait them a long while beforehand and then lie hid in the bushes ahead of time till they came down as usual and then let fly at 'em and get your meat. Izzy had noticed a large hollow black-gum log lying at the edge of the cornfield with its open end pointing out to the field. The tree had been cut down many years before for a bee-tree. So he did some thinking and planning. He got a shovel and dug a long v-shaped trench leading from the log out into the field, and into this trench he scattered a peck of shelled corn. At first nothing happened. When he went down during the first day after, the corn was untouched, and then a day or two later he saw it was being eaten and crow tracks were all around in the soft dirt. He replenished the grain with another peck. The next time he went down, a great flock of crows flew up out of the ditch before he got within two hundred yards of the place. He put in still more corn, and for two weeks or so he continued to do so. Then one morning long before day he felt the time had come. He got up long before daybreak to put his plan into execution. His father heard him stirring about and asked him what he was up to.

"I'm going after them crows," Izzy said. "And a silver quarter for each dead one—right?"

"Right," said his daddy, "and it ain't gonna cost me a cent, baiting or no baiting."

"They've been eating that shelled corn right hearty lately," said Izzy, "and I expect there's mergins of 'em. I'll come back later and get the wagon to haul 'em in—after you hear my muzzle-loader go off down there in the field."

"You and *my* muzzle-loader," said his daddy, "and I'll bet you five dollars to a nickel you don't kill crow one."

"I'll take the bet," said Izzy. "Shake?" and they did.

"You'll never get close enough to 'em," said his pa. "You can hide in the bushes but they'll see you."

"Wanter make another bet I can't hide where they don't see me?" said Izzy.

"Go on with your bets, boy, and be careful not to load that gun too heavy, it'll kick your teeth out."

"I reckon I've shot it plenty times," said Izzy. He went out into the kitchen and there by lamplight loaded it. And a big extra load of powder and a handful of Number 4 shot he put into each barrel and rammed them home with double wadding. Yes, sir, the crows better watch out this time. And he hurried off across the fields in the dark. Reaching the hollow log, he backed inside it, and propped his muzzle-loader all capped and cocked, with the barrels pointing straight down the trench where the supply of corn shone white and waiting for the crows. He put a scattering of twigs and little brush stuff in front of his face, and there he lay all camouflaged and snug peering out, waiting.

Just as daylight was beginning to show, the crows started arriving. And crows, crows! Never had Izzy seen so many. And they kept coming and lighting down, cawing away, flapping their wings, dipping their heads down and up, down and up, guzzling away at the corn. Before long the v-shaped trench, some hundred or more feet long, was jammed full of them. Now was the time! Izzy sighted carefully down along the seam between the barrels of the old muzzle-loader, aiming full along the trench. Then he pulled both triggers.

Up at the house Mr. and Mrs. Izzard were having early breakfast when the sound of the gun was heard. The three other children were still asleep.

"Well, Izzy finally has shot at something down there in the fields," Norman said.

"Seemed like it sounded mighty loud, don't you think so, Norman?"

"Well, it did for a fact," he said, as he reached for another flapjack. "He'll be on in a minute and I'll collect that bet out of him from his tin box. I bet him five dollars he wouldn't kill crow one."

"I hope nothing's happened," his wife said.

"Nothing can happen to Izzy," Norman said and laughed. "You know what he said, he said he'd come get the two-horse wagon to haul up the dead crows. Hah, hah!"

Time passed. The three children were up and out at play. Norman milked the cows, came in and helped his wife clean up things. But Izzy hadn't shown up.

"Maybe you'd better go down there and see if anything's happened," Mrs. Izzard said.

He set out across the field, and when he came to the edge of the new ground piece where Izzy had baited the birds, he saw a sight the like of which he'd never seen before. Dead crows were lying in piles on top of one another, the long ditch full of them, and a few crippled ones were flopping about, trying to fly or walk. Norman looked anxiously around for Izzy. "Izzy, Izzy, where are you!" he called. But no Izzy. He stood there thinking, and then he put two and two together and figured the shot that killed the crows had come from the edge of the woods there. He walked over and saw the half-concealed end of hollow log, and he saw something else. He saw Izzy's limp arm lying there in the opening of the log across the barrel of the old muzzle-loader. In no time he had dragged the boy out of there and into the sunlight.

Izzy seemed dead to the world, and blood was seeping out of both his ears. "Izzy, Izzy," his daddy called, and rolled him back and forth. Finally Izzy opened his eyes and asked what happened. He didn't hear what his daddy said for he was deaf as a post. The concussion of the gun inside the log had really clobbered him. Out in the air it would only have given him a hard kick but inside the log and with the extra heavy loads of powder and shot, the shock waves had almost killed him. His daddy spoke to him again, but Izzy couldn't hear a word. And for several days he was deaf as could be.

But what did Izzy care, for he had really massacred the crows. Just as he had said, they had to get the two-horse wagon to haul them in, and they put them in a great heap in front of the house to show the astounded neighbors and the wondering children. By count there were 879 crows, including the few crippled ones he and his daddy killed with a stick. And true to his words Norman paid up the full amount at a quarter a crow which with the five dollar bet came to $224.75. Izzy took it all over to the bank in town and opened a savings account. By this time he could hear again.

"Ah, that Izzy," the neighbors said, "ain't he something! He'll be a millionaire someday and even maybe governor of the state."

"Or who knows," said another, "maybe president. I wouldn't put nothing past him."

But Izzy never became the man they prophesied. Perhaps the concussion inside the log had addled his brains, I don't know. But for one reason or another he never amounted to much. Until he died, a poor farmer, the big day in his life was the day he murdered a mass of crows. For that the Valley remembers him.

White Swelling

As a little boy I suffered with it for two terrible years. I first fell out of an apple tree and hurt my arm, and then the disease took over. Many a night I would lie in front of the fire on a pallet with my aching arm and knee toward the soothing heat, and every hour or two my mother would rise from her bed and put on replenishing logs. Dr. Joe McKay treated me with every kind of purgative known to man, including calomel, black draught, and castor oil.

Every passing neighbor prescribed remedies too. "I'll tell you what, Billy," one would say to my father, "get you some red oak bark, bile it good and mix the tea with meal and make a good poultice, then wrop that boy's arm in it, and it'll do the trick." Another would say, "His kidneys are poisoning him. Feed him some of this good swamp root and he'll mend right away." Swamp root was one of the hundreds of patent medicines for which the hardworking people in the Valley paid out their good money to the medical scavengers. Finally Dr. Joe lost patience with me and one day in his little office there in Buies Creek where I had gone for treatment, he had his Negro man grab me and hold me. "Look out yonder and see that crow, Paul," he said. I looked off, and pang! he had split my elbow open with his lancet. Then, as the Negro continued to hold my churning form, the doctor progued in my inner forearm with a huge sucking needle. I still bear the scars and I still hear in my inner ear the awful screams I let out.

"Billy," he said later to my father, "you better take him

up to Johns Hopkins in Baltimore to Dr. Osler and let him cut his arm off. He's going to die if you don't and that soon." Somehow my father and mother scraped up $75 and Father took me to Baltimore and just in time, for although I was ten years old I weighed less than forty pounds. The wonderful doctors at the hospital saved both me and my arm.

Old Aunt Margaret Messer, Little Bethel Church's holy woman, opposed my going to the last. "Prayer is the only thing that will save him, prayer and Dr. Yokum's sanctified handkerchiefs put on the pizen place," she said. I am glad my parents wouldn't listen to her.

So I have some definite opinions on the subject of white swelling. So has my old friend Mr. Mac, the miller. One day when I was down at his mill chewing the rag with him on various matters, folklorish, historical and sundry, Ashe Brodie, the bootlegger, came in with a peck of corn to be ground. He was wiv-wavering with drunkenness, and Mr. Mac fell afoul of him for his ways and especially for having his sick son down to the Holy Roller camp meeting at Falcon to be prayed over and healed of his bone disease by the sanctified people.

"Why in the world, Ashe," the old miller fumed, "don't you take that boy up to Rex Hospital and get him operated on for that leg that's rotting off?" But the slobbering hypocrite whined and said he was ashamed of Mr. Mac for not putting his trust more in the power of "our almighty and blessed Lord." Ashe himself was almost a nervous wreck from hiding in the swamps and jumping from every wind-moving bush, fearing it was a revenue officer. And while the old miller had him there hemmed up in the millhouse, he worked a bit on his sorry superstitious soul—for that crippled boy's sake.

"Ashe," he said, "you better be careful how you mix your medicine and your Lord. They're like oil and water. You ain't old enough, but I remember the case of Tatum Baker, the liquor-head. He woke up one morning with his back bent like a jackknife. Some said a spell had been put on him, others that he slept without a sheet and had caught the cramps. Anyhow, he went for months like that. He tried all kinds of quack doctors, plasters, pills and even took a case or two of female disorder medicine, but nothing seemed to help him. Finally he gave in to his wife's pleading and went down to the Holiness meeting at Falcon to be prayed over.

"And the sisters and brothers prayed all right—for a night and the whole of the next day they did. About sundown of the second day, the misery left Tatum, and he straightened up and went to shouting. Not only that, but he happy-danced off a piece up and down the church aisle, and let loose a great bellowing of unknown tongues. Yessir, he was healed and healed good. He thought he was. But old Moster was only playing with him. He had to celebrate. He stopped there in Dunn and got himself a quart of liquor and drank it all as he walked on home. This time wouldn't count, he said, just the way all you liquor-heads say, and before long he was addled and drunk as he wobbled ahead.

"It was a hot night and a big thundercloud had come up. As he wandered up the lane at the Shovel place, a real cloudburst fell out of the sky. Now it happened that old Andrew Shovel himself was lying dead in his house. Some neighbors were there sitting up, and in front of his yard was a hearse with its two black-plumed horses tied to a tree. Tatum hurried along as fast as he could, and as he got near, in his disordered state of mind, he mistook the hearse for some sort of covered carriage. Since it was pouring such a heavy rain and thundering and lightning so bad he opened the door and crawled in to keep dry.

"Now as everybody knows, a hearse don't have any handles on the inside, for the corpse has no need to open the door from within. Well, all of a sudden and blam! the lightning struck a tree in old Shovel's yard. The horses bucked and charged and broke loose, and away they went back toward Dunn where they came from. As they went charging along, and the hearse whooming and blundering from side to side, Tatum's mind cleared up somewhat and he realized where he was. And then he set up a terrible yelling and screeching and praying to the Lord God Almighty —sort of the way you must have done the other day, Ashe, when you were trying to get saved at the mourners' bench—yeh, no doubt just the way you did.

"Other neighbors heard the sound of the horses and the hearse coming, and they rushed out on their porches as it went by. And in the flashes of lightning they could see the 'dead man' in there, squatted on his knees, throwing up his hands and bowing and praying. And they fled back inside and barred their doors. Finally the horses ran smack into the main avenue of Dunn, and there by the street lights the inhabitants visioned this strange flying contraption. And more than one of them bolted out of the house and took to the alleys and side streets and even fields. Right on through the town the horses ran. And as they swerved around the curve going toward Clinton, the hearse turned over and threw Tatum out through the broken glass and hard against a ditch stump. This time he really was hurt. His back was cracked.

"From that day forth he walked exactly as he walked before—bent all over—and neither doctors nor preachers could ever heal him. They said he learned his lesson all right, but he learned it too late. For before long he died a lost soul from liquor—hardening of the liver and in great pain. No sir, it won't do to mix your medicine and your religion.

"Now sit still, Ashe, for that ain't all, and you know where there's no hope there's no hurry and many a man feeds his brains to his belly. Take the case of another bootlegger like you—bootlegger, you heard me, Ashe—old man Abner Witherspoon, who had denied his children both their chance at health and schooling, all for the sake of the liquor he loved. He once got down mighty low with locked bowels, and he promised the good God if he would let him up again he would serve him all the days of his life, would take care of his wife and children, never make whiskey again, never curse, and never have evil thoughts rambling in his brain. So God let him up, and he walked about. But it weren't any time at all till he was back at that whiskey still, firing and straining and a-cussing and thinking of every Saturday night when he'd get off down to Dunn and cut up with some hot wild women. You know how it was, Ashe, for you do that yourself, married man though you be. So God Almighty struck him down again and brought him right to the hinge creak of the gate of death. And such a loud clamoring and powwow of praying and begging the country had never heard before. Sort of like the powwowing and hollering you did the other day, Ashe, from what they tell me. Maybe it was because of these children and his wife, Melinda, a godly woman all the years of her being, that the Big Boss in the sky finally heard him again and restored him to health.

"What did he do then? He did what so many of us are prone to do—and what you have done time and again, Ashe—the minute the threat of danger faded far away, he went back to his vomit. But as the squealing hog said when the devil sheared him, once is a lot, two times is too much, and three times is completely and tee-totally overdoing it. So for old Abner there never was a third chance. For when he started back consorting with Old Scratch—and you know every time a man falls he falls harder than before and mires up that much deeper in the slough of his undoing—well, the ha'nts got him this time. Yessir, and I mean ha'nts. You can call it delirium tremens, the happy weepings or the jerks or the pentecostal pourings, but anyhow old Abner was a pitiful sight to see. You know how it is, Ashe, when you begin to see faces in knotholes and hear voices in your head and little fingers begin tickling behind your ears, and a great creature you can't even see begins to walk behind you with heavy feet, and you hear him going bump, bump all in time to your beating heart.

"One day the Iron-faced Man would be after Abner. Then another day Raw-head-and-Bloody-bones would run him around the house. Then at night likely as not the little Headless Girl would get under his bed and snigger at him with gurgling sounds coming up from the slit place in her throat. Be still, Ashe, I ain't finished.

"Then there was the ghost of old Aunt Mahaly the witch woman, with her bucket of snakes, that would get after him. She would set upon him in his delirium, coming up out of the deep Cape Fear swamps to do it, with Jack-muh-Lantern coming ahead of her with a ball of fox fire in his hand to light her way. And she would bring her witch's pot and put it right in the middle of the floor and start her fire burning around her devil's brew, and the snakes crawling out of the bucket would get busy bringing chips in their mouths to feed the fire. He thought they did—he was so far gone.

"And it was right there that the wonderworking ways of nature's God took his final reckoning with Abner. For one night when the thunder and lightning were popping and cracking in the trees around the house, the ha'nt of old Aunt Mahaly started her hocus-pocus by his bed, snakes and all. Some of the neighbors were sitting up with him that night and trying to hold him down. The next day Finley Broom was coming to haul him away to the asylum. But when morning broke coolish and fair with the world all fresh and clean again, there was no need of Finley's straight-jacket and his buggy. For during the night old Abner had got loose from his neighbors and jumped spang in the middle of Aunt Mahaly's boiling bubbling washpot and was scalded to death. Yessir, Ashe, it's not what actually is in the world that makes so much to-do with man, but what he thinks is in the world. Scalded to death, you heard me.

"From the squallings and babble of words that had kept

breaking from old Abner's lips as he died, the watchers knew he thought it was boiling water into which he leapt. Anyhow more than one swore that when they picked him up from the floor dead as a nit he had blisters on his hands and face same as if actual scalding water had been poured on him. Take it or leave it, that's what they said. Heigh, wait a minute, Ashe, don't rush off like that. I'm just getting to the point."

But Ashe was gone out of the millhouse as if the dogs were after him, and he raised a dust fleeing down the road. Mr. Mac must have scared him some, for he did do right by his crippled boy the next day—sent him to a surgeon at Rex Hospital and had him finally cured of his white swelling. But for Ashe there seems to be no cure. He is back again making liquor in the swamp and drinking plentifully of it, and trembling and moaning with nervousness every time a pine cone falls.

Baptizing

The favorite baptizing place for our Pleasant Union Church was the old Reuben Matthews millpond some four miles above Buies Creek on the way to Angier. It was there I was baptized as an eleven-year-old boy after my fake conversion in the church, and I remember that baptizing day vividly too. I was so self-conscious and sure that everybody was looking at me and no one else that even as the preacher led the line of us—boys and girls, men and women—into the chilly water the embarrassed sweat was pouring out and over my body.

But as sweaty and troubled as I was I couldn't help noticing how the young women, dressed in black stockings and in dark dresses, kept turning loose a partner's hand to push down their air-billowing skirts into the water for modesty's sake as they solemnly proceeded, and I saw too that the men on the bank, including the deacons, were watching these girls and nobody else. And when poor Cissie Ochiltree's skirt got lifted way up by the imprisoned air, I heard a boy, Grover Gregory by name, standing on the bank, give a sharp brash snicker at the sight of her white drawers, and the men on the bank chuckled out loud too.

All the while Preacher Wicker with his tall cudgel feeling for holes ahead of him was leading us on into the water. When he had got where the pond was about waist deep or a little more, he began the business of baptizing us, taking us one by one. With his hand behind the convert's head, and his other hand on the shoulder, he would sing out in a high rolling chant, "I baptize thee, Sister Luvenie, in the name of the Father and of the Son and of the Holy Ghost—Amen!" And then swoosh and down under he would douse the sister, and she would usually come up sputtering and squealing and spitting water, and with her hair hanging wet and in strings over her shoulders.

Again, Cissie had trouble when she was put under. She swallowed a gulletful of water and came up belching and vomiting suds, mad as a wet hen. "You nigh 'bout drownded me, that's what you done!" she squalled to the preacher, and she started to claw at him. But Eddie Maxton reached out and stopped her and quieted her. And he kept his arm sort of soft and comforting about her as he waited. Cissie was a rather pretty plump girl, and now with her wet clothes stuck tight to her, everybody, including Eddie and the men on the bank and me too, could see how her breastworks stood out big and round. (Breastworks was only one of the many terms we boys in our secret sex discussions used to designate women's bosoms.)

And now Preacher Wicker had to call Eddie by name to get his attention from Cissie and let him know he was next in line for the cleansing waters—waters which by this time were beginning to get rather muddy. It occurred to me then that maybe Eddie was like me, still unregenerate for all this show and no more saved than I was, and the thought gave me comfort. Later, events at the sawmill showed this was true. After his conversion and his short spell as a Christian, Eddie never seemed able to get up steam in the old boiler the way he could when he was spouting tobacco juice and his volleys of profanity at the iron creature. I heard Mr. Joe Johnson who owned the raggle-taggle mill say that one morning a few days later when he got there about daylight the old steam valve was already popping off and Eddie was chewing tobacco and cussing happily away as of old as he crammed the fat turpentine-butted outsides into the firebox, and he, Mr. Joe, was glad to see that Eddie had gone back to his old life, bad as it was to say so.

When my turn came with Preacher Wicker, I was in better command of myself. The water had carried off my sweat and cooled my body. I still remember how he pushed me way down and under, and I heard a great roaring as he held me there awhile for the final washing away of my sins. But I saved my breath and was ready to pop to the surface when he lightened his grasp, and so I was in good command of things and spat no water at all. Later I began to wonder if he hadn't punished me a bit extra for the effort he had had to put forth to get me into the fold and so had kept me under longer than was fair.

As with Eddie Maxton, my "salvation"—if you could call it that—didn't last. I had no tobacco or profanity to go back to, but I had my reading and my frank and free poetry to work at, and I more and more began to look on the local church and the preachers there as pretty much fakes and phonies. Two or three years later I had a chance to get a bit of revenge on them, not much but a bit. I was growing into the gosling stage and was full of prankish fancies and a lot of thinking about girls.

At the baptizing that year in the same pond, Grover Gregory and I climbed up into the top storey of the old mill-house and there secreted ourselves by the open attic window with beanshooters and a supply of little BB shot and had great glee in letting fly at the assemblage below. We concentrated especially on the girls who were being baptized and whose tight wet garments got better results for us. We would carefully raise our heads above the windowsill, lift our shooters, and send a soundless little pellet on its way, then jook down and wait awhile before the next furtive shot. The girls kept jumping and twitching and slapping themselves, thinking all the while, as we knew they would, that horseflies and dogflies, usually bad at that time of the year, were after them. When Grover and I had tormented them to our full satisfaction, we got in a few stinging pings on the preacher and his wet clothes. After this we crept quietly down the stairway and in a few minutes appeared among the congregation straight-faced and solemn as any true men of God might be on a holy Sabbath morning.

That was the last baptism I ever attended. Sometime after this I found me a country sweetheart who loved poetry or said she did—and she later proved it in many a hushed and fervent hour. And from then on for a long while romantic dreams and pouring images and rhythms held me in thrall as I labored on my father's farm. And Sunday after Sunday my horse or mule would be tied to a tree in front of her house. And inside the house in the parlor she and I would be soul-sharing the beauties of Tennyson or Wordsworth or Keats or Shelley—or the somber measures of Edgar Poe's "Ulalume" or "King Death," or even discussing in fervent intimacy the plots of Mary J. Holmes's novels or the burning passion of Mrs. E. D. E. N. Southworth's *Ishmael.* And then another Sunday it was the bursting racial cry of Thomas Dixon's *The Clansman.*

But the novels were soon used up, the poetry never. It was always more and still more, and on to Shakespeare—

> Take, O take those lips away,
> That so sweetly were forsworn,
> And those eyes the break of day,
> Lights that do mislead the morn—

Tears, idle tears, I now know what they mean!

How Needham Jones Became a Preacher

Over the years I have known many preachers who have come and gone in the Valley, and without exception they all declared they became preachers because God had called them. And I must say that almost without exception too, God showed mighty poor judgment in his selection. I remember the example of Needham Jones, though the final results as to him I must agree were not bad at all.

This Needham was a lonely, plowhandle sort of fellow, timid and of few words indeed. Maybe in his very lonesomeness in the wide fields he felt the need of comfort and so developed some kind of closeness to his God. Anyway, he confided to his sister Lida one night at the table—the two of them lived alone in their little farmhouse after their parents' death—that something strange had happened to him that day as he was plowing. He heard a voice clear as a bell say, "Needham, I want you to preach." Lida looked at him in astonishment, saying he might as well get that wild idea out of his head. It must have been something he et, she said, or maybe he was like that Victor Blalock fellow that thought he heard God saying "Go preach, go preach!" only to find out later that it was Heck Turner's old jackass sounding off.

And to add to Needham's other disabilities he at times stuttered badly. But as the devout people in the Valley say and have said for generations, "The Lord moves in mysterious ways his wonders to perform."

It happened sometime after that that an old Negro woman who had once been a cotton hoe-hand for Needham's father died, and the Negro preacher came over and invited Needham and Lida to the funeral, saying, "Aunt Hy'cinth loved yo' daddy and she sho' would 'preciate yo' 'tendance." So Needham and his sister went to the funeral in the nearby Negro meeting house. It was a bitterly cold day and a big fire was going in the iron heater in the crowded church. Much to Needham's dismay the preacher came down the aisle, got him by the hand, and the next thing he and Lida knew they were wedged in on the front seat and cut off from the door by an aisle full of Negro mourners and relatives who were crowding in. Caught fast, he sat there in a cold sweat between the congregation and Aunt Hyacinth's black cloth-covered pine coffin.

Then the preacher started his funeral sermon on Aunt Hyacinth, and much to Needham's surprise made it quiet and short. But he wasn't so surprised long, for the reverend explained that there was one with them this day who would speak words of sympathy and praise about the "deceasted." Poor timid Needham shuddered where he sat and a great silent groan went up inside him as the preacher pointed to him and called his name. Lida nudged him and whispered that he at least ought to stand up and be recognized. A great "Amen, Brother," sounded from the congregation in urgent expectancy. Needham finally got to his feet and stuttered out a word or two about old Aunt Hyacinth being a fine character and mighty good with a hoe. Before he could sink back into his seat more loud cries of "Amen" broke out and others were added, "You tell it, Brother," "Amen," "Listen to the word!"

"Go on, go on," Lida urged, even pushing him from behind. "Say a little bit more—they expect it."

So all bent over and ready to sit down again, Needham managed another word or two and the amens and hallelujahs began to grow more numerous and loud. The preacher now stepped down from the little pulpit, as Needham was taking his seat, got the poor timid fellow by the arm and pulled him firmly out toward the coffin. Then he began clapping his hands and whooping things along in encouragement.

Needham managed to squeeze out a few more words, and the preacher moved to one side out of the way, sat down, and left him in charge. The congregation kept calling on him to tell the good news about Aunt Hyacinth. "Preach her on into Abraham's bosom," they pleaded loudly.

The terrific emotional upheaval now going on in Needham caused something to happen. He started talking more freely, and the Negroes started answering him with the 'sponse. And every time he'd weaken or stutter they'd roll in with their hallelujahs and amens and sweep him on.

Finally he got going, and soon he was walking the floor, pacing unafraid about the coffin, his eyes flashing, his long plowhandle arms weaving like winding blades in a flood of drumming words pouring from his lips.

"You know not the day nor the hour!" he shouted. And the wild 'sponse rolled back from the congregation—"Preach it, brother, preach it on up to the gates of glory."

And they say he did. Never had such a funeral service been preached in Hickory Grove Church as Needham Jones preached that day.

From then on he was a preacher, and one of the best, and he was never known to stutter again. He went on the road bringing sinners to Christ. He quit farming in the hot sunlit fields, for he took literally the words of the Biblical preacher who said, "What profit hath a man of all his labor wherein he laboreth under the sun?" So he left his farm, and Lida hired a foolish boy, Erse Harmon, to help farm in his stead. Later she married Erse and the two are doing well. Needham is still traveling up and down the Valley as far as Wilmington to the south and east and Greensboro to the north, thundering forth the word of God. Now and then you can hear his hoarse hasseling voice over the Sunday morning radio. But he is getting old now and his powers against the Devil and all his works are weakening.

The Contrarious Man

"I have known many contrarious men in my time," said old Luke Pemberton as I was having lunch with him in the Prince Charles Hotel in Fayetteville one day, "but Plunkett Barksdale was the most contrarious."

I had been snooping up and down the Valley on one of my folk-tale and anecdote gatherings and had stopped in town and asked old Luke to join me for lunch, hoping to get a story or two about the old days out of him, and now I was to get one.

"Plunkett was a high-living fellow," he went on, "and inherited right much money and land from his daddy Fifer Bill Barksdale up there near Smith's Ferry. But as time passed and he begun to get on in years, he joined the local Damascus Church. Of course, there was a lot of jubilation over that—at first there was.

"Like so many Scotchmen, Plunkett had a high temper and was mighty contrarious and touchous, as I said. For some reason or other—some say it was over hogs, others over a land boundary—he quarreled with one of the church elders named Merlin McTaggert. The two had a lawsuit before the J. P. and the case was decided against Plunkett. Later he attacked Merlin in the road one day with a stick and whipped him. Both men were had up in the church for fighting, and again the case was proved against Plunkett. The brethren waited on him and said he would have to publicly apologize to Merlin and get the Lord's forgiveness before he was allowed to return to good standing in the congregation. Plunkett said he wouldn't do it. And he didn't, and he harbored a grudge against all the members from then on.

"His spite took a funny shape. He went off and joined the Catholic Church, where as he said, a man could drink now and then, dance if he wanted to, and get justice done him. But that wasn't all. He moseyed around among some of his former cronies and organized a meeting house of his own. Now one of these rounders happened to own the land close to Damascus Church, just to the other side of it. So Plunkett bought a couple of acres and put up a church of his own. It wasn't much of a building, but it was good enough for Plunkett and his followers and had a cross set above it.

"I don't guess it really was a Catholic Church. Plunkett just called it that to spite the Damascus Presbyterian folks. Anyway some few rambunctious services were held there with him doing the reading, and it might have grown into something if it had stood long enough. But in a year or two somebody burnt it down. Soon after it was burnt, Plunkett was taken down sick, some said from too much carousing and others said from the grippe he caught the night his church burnt, when he overdid himself fighting the fire. He was taken with double pneumonia, and nothing could be done to save him.

Just before he died he called all his buddies in and said he wanted them not to grieve after him and be sad and mournful like most church funerals and wakes. No, he wanted them to be joyful. He said he was getting plenty of hard liquor and a big jug of cherry bounce ordered for them all and they must make merry around his coffin and corpse before they carried him across the creek and buried him there where his church had stood. I suppose he still wanted to plague the Damascus people, for his grave would be there where they could look out the window and see it all lonely and unjustly treated by itself. He ordered a copper casket too from the Lauder people here, into which he was to be put, and a whole barrel of brandy was to be poured in around him to keep him pickled for generations. That would worry the deacons some and would bother that old reformed teetotaler Merlin McTaggert no little as he was singing his hymns there in the amen-corner and looking through the window and thinking of him, Plunkett, out there lying in a sea of good liquor.

"Plunkett died and the funeral parlor people from Fayetteville put him in the casket, poured in the brandy as had been agreed, and welded him up as instructed.

"Then the wake began, and what a wake it was: For a night and day his old companions drank and held watch over him, with some singing and laughing and cutting up even. In the afternoon of the second day they started with the corpse toward the church. The weather was bad for burying anybody, even Plunkett. A terrible flood of winter rain had fallen all mixed with sleet and snow, and when the burying party came to Slocumb's Creek they found the bridge washed away and gone. So they stopped and held a caucus. They were all pretty drunk and they come near to blows as to what to do. Finally they decided to go down the stream a little way where some trees had been blown across the run in the year of the hurricane and try to make their way across with the body. So they did.

"What with the sleet on the slippery logs and their being half-drunk, these cronies fell into the creek, casket and all. The bank was steep there and a lot of jagged rocks stuck out from the sides. The casket fell against some of these rocks and rolled down into the water. For a while it seemed Plunkett would be washed down the stream and into the Cape Fear River to be lost to the fishes at sea, but with a lot of shouting and hullabaloo they finally got him up the bank and onto the other side. Then they found that the casket had been cracked from the rough handling and a gurgle of fine brandy was pouring out. For a while they tried to stop up the leak. But finally seeing it couldn't be done and the brandy would be wasted, they decided that Plunkett wouldn't mind. So they fell to catching it in their hats and drinking it like pigs. When the brandy was all leaked out or drunk up, they started on toward the churchyard, and where they had been half-drunk before, they were all roaring drunk now. And they sang all kinds of ballads and dirty songs as they staggered along. Neighborhood people heard them a-doing it and shook their heads at the shame.

"When they got to the burial place with the casket they hardly knew B from bull's foot. So it was that in their addled condition they couldn't see straight and so dug Plunkett's grave and buried him not straight east and west as decent people should be buried but slanchindicular, catty-cornered like, that is contrarious, as you might say. And maybe this was a fitting thing to do, seeing that he was so like that in life.

"Later there was talk of digging Plunkett up and moving

him. But for one reason or another it was put off, and finally the whole thing was forgot, and today trees and bushes cover the place where he lies all gentle and subdued."

Austin Honey and the Buzzards

The story of Austin Honey and his struggle with the buzzards has long been a fireside tale in the Cape Fear River Valley.

Austin was from hardy God-fearing Scotch stock. He ran a small farm and tended fish traps on the rapids of the Cape Fear, and like many a good Scotchman in that section he was a stubborn fellow, and he had to be to make a living from his sandy acres and these traps.

He was not only God-fearing and stubborn but a bit miserly and grasping for the pence. It was this last trait more than any other perhaps which led to his downfall. In his haste to get his fish out of the traps and up into Summerville before the other fishermen got there, he slubbered his work. If he happened to find a catch of red rock or bass or shad floundering in the foaming waters that poured through the slats in his traps, he would haul these fish out and into his sack and toss the unsalable mud cats and suckers carelessly aside. Some of these culls fell on the rocks and spoiled there in the sun.

Uncle Josh, the old colored man who ran the ferry below the falls and made shad nets in his spare time, said to him, "Mr. Austin, you better clean up them there dead fish. If you don't you'll like as not start the buzzards to using around here. And everybody knows a buzzard is a plumb dirty mess and tribulation." But Austin didn't listen.

And the great black scavengers began to settle down out of the sky and eat the dead stinking fish. From eating the dead ones they finally began to steal the live ones out of the traps. Then it was that the economical soul of Austin Honey got fired up.

He was a member of good standing in the Little Bethel Church and sometimes even taught the Sunday school class there. So, remembering his pride of place, he controlled himself and refrained from violent language. But one morning when he came down to the river and found a half-dozen of the big ungainly birds sitting around gorged to the gills, their wrinkled bald heads nodding in the sun and his traps completely empty, he flew into sudden and spontaneous profanity and cursed them to a fare you well.

Uncle Josh, sitting on the bank of the river snoozing under a sycamore tree, said to him, "That's mighty pow'ful language you's a-using for a good church member, Mr. Austin, ain't it, suh?"

Austin acknowledged it was and felt properly ashamed. As the days went by the number of buzzards kept increasing, and it looked as if the main means of his livelihood would be destroyed. They had really developed a sweet tooth for the live fish by this time. But he was a man and held his tongue in. He went off to the hardware store and bought himself a shotgun on a credit, and fired after and around the birds to frighten them. They soon got on to the sham shooting and ignored him. Then on a day he lost his temper and fired in among them, killing several. He should have known better, for the local law in those days was stern on such matters.

He was promptly hailed before the justice of the peace and fined five dollars for each of the dead birds. He explained his case to the judge. And his jackleg lawyer, Hopping June Harris, pleaded and moved and objected, but no go. His Honor was hard-boiled—for he suspected Austin of shortchanging him on a roe shad recently—and so Austin in a rage had to accept the verdict and pay up.

Then he did like many a troubled man before him. He sought refuge in whiskey. Straight across the street to the dispensary he went, and came out an hour later sod-drunk. He began to harangue the air against the judge and quite a crowd collected around him on the street corner. Finally he began to let out a lot of threats, and so there was nothing to do but lock him up. And he spent the night in jail.

For this scandalous behavior the deacons and elders of Little Bethel Church called him before them and warned him to mend his ways. He told them that if they would keep the buzzards from his traps, he would. They couldn't promise that, so he refused to repent. And they expelled him.

After that Austin quit church and Sunday school altogether. As time passed he went to the bad with profanity, blasphemous language, and liquor. But he never relaxed his stubborn contest with the buzzards, drunk or sober, nor they with him. If he rose and came to the traps in the dawn, they were there before him. When he sat up at night they sat up too. When he slept they robbed him. And when he woke they fled from him.

One winter night he staggered to his traps with his lantern to find one of the finest openmouthed bass he'd ever seen being lifted in a buzzard's beak, and he rushed forward with a yell loud enough to wake Uncle Josh in his shack up on the hill. He struck at the buzzard with his lantern, and because he was a little wobbly on his legs from his overheavy slug of whiskey—in fact he was never sober anymore—he missed the buzzard and went head over heels, lantern and all, into a deep swirling whirlpool below the falls. He came near drowning, but finally he beat his way down to a willow clump on a little island some several hundred yards below the rapids. And there he stayed, chilled and freezing to the bone until Uncle Josh and the neighbors rescued him.

A few days after this he developed a case of double pneumonia. And by the end of the week it was spoken around among the neighbors that Austin Honey was going to die, and buzzards were the cause.

Then he did a queer thing. He summoned several friends to his bedside. "Folks," he quavered piteously, and with heavy breathing—"folks, it looks like they've about done for me—them buzzards I mean." And his glazed sick eyes rested dolorously on their sympathetic faces.

"Yes, Austin," they said, "it's all too bad." Then they sat silent, for they were God-fearing people, and they thought he had summoned them to pray for him that his wickedness might be forgiven and he be made ready to pass over the cold river of death into the promised land above. And they were all in a prayerful mood. But never a word about praying did he speak.

"I've got a dying request to make of you," he said hoarsely —"a dying request. And you know that the wishes of the dead are sacred." They nodded agreement that this was so. "Then listen to me," he went on waveringly, "and do what I tell you. When I'm dead, and it won't be long, I want you to take me up on yon hill by the river above my fish traps—" and he pointed with a trembling finger through the window toward the hill in the distance—"and bury me there right on the top of it, out in the field space. And I want you to put me in an open coffin, with the lid off. You hear me? Do you?"

"Yes, Austin, we hear you," they said.

"And you'll do what I say!"

They finally agreed. And with burning insistence he made them put their hands on the big Bible and swear to it.

"When you've done that," he went on, "and got me there in that open coffin I want you to build some hard and fast brickwork up over me and around me—pen me in like. Jake there knows what I mean—the way he done Mr. Sexton's front yard wall. Tough and strong I want it. But leave good-sized cracks between the bricks, you understand me." The ragged breathing of the sick man was touching to hear.

"Yes," said Jake sadly and gravely, "you want us to sort of dodge the bricks."

"Yeh, dodge 'em, that's what I mean," whispered Austin.

"What in the world you want that for?" said Marvin Whittaker, the blacksmith.

"No matter what I want it for," Austin coughed painfully and even angrily, "I want it. And I want the cracks between them there bricks big enough so you can look through and see me there lying peaceful-like in my coffin."

"I believe his wits is a-wandering," said old Phinny Barlow, the cow doctor.

"Wits!" wheezed Austin. "You fools wait and see." And he beat the bed on either side with his dying, angry fists.

Soon after that Austin died. And Jake and his friends, even as they had promised, performed the last sad rites for their dead friend. They set him in an open coffin on top of the hill. And a good stout interlaced structure of brickwork was built up over and around him and mortared well.

The next morning when Jake Senter looked up toward the hill he saw a single buzzard sitting on the brick death house. And a little later in the day he noticed a second buzzard had arrived and joined the first, and by sunset time a flock of them was slowly wheeling in the sky. The following morning quite a number of them were wandering around there on top of the hill. Some were sitting on the latticework and others were poking their heads in through the open spaces between the bricks.

But none of them could get at Austin. None at all. And there he lay serene in his open coffin protected from their reach by the stout bricks. All day long more buzzards were arriving from every direction, north, south, east, and west.

And early in the morning of the third day the people from the town could see the hill literally black with them.

And then the fun really began. Too bad that Austin couldn't see it. A terrific struggle of buzzard muscle and brawn took place against bricks and stout concrete. Singly and in pairs and in a flock these great black birds would go after Austin. And then they began to fight among themselves for the privilege of another try at him. They beat their old wrinkled heads bloody against the bricks, they wore the feathers away from their rawbony shoulders. And day and night they kept at it. For a fortnight or so the struggle went on, and all the while more buzzards were landing in the scene.

In their way they were just as stubborn as Austin had been in his. They wouldn't give up. And as the days went by they drooped and sickened by the hundreds. Their frustration and disappointment brought them into a lethargy of prostration and breakdown. They began to die in droves. Also starvation and efforts at mutual cannibalism took toll of them where they carried on their ceaseless and futile toil. All over the hill you could see them scattered like humped bunches of black rags where they lay dead with the dust blowing and sifting over them.

Some said there was no doubt of it at all—Austin Honey soon would have cleaned the birds out of the Cape Fear Valley as well as all of North Carolina maybe and had a final and complete revenge if the wind hadn't changed. But it did, and began to blow down back toward the village. That was too much for decent folks living there. And when finally they could stand it no longer the more hardy and self-respecting ones fastened wet vinegar cloths to their noses with clothespins and went up to the top of the hill with shovels and mattocks. They raked away the great piles of dead buzzards, tore down the brickwork, closed up the coffin, dug a grave there on the spot, and put Austin reverently and definitely in it.

And any time now you go along that road, folks will point out to you the place where Austin Honey was buried long ago—him that had such a fight with the buzzards. And the name of that hill to this day is Buzzard Hill.

Excursion

It was a bright day in Spring and I had gone with my father to the neighboring town of Angier to get a load of fertilizer for our farm. I was eleven then, and as always was anxious to see the train come in. And while my father was down at the siding getting the fertilizer loaded onto the wagon, I stood by the little passenger station waiting for the train. Several others were waiting there too, among them a crippled, old Confederate soldier still wearing his gray military cap and leaning on his walking stick. Soon the locomotive showed its round black moon of a face with its brass trimmings turning the bend. It was an old woodburner and puffed and wheezed along till it finally drew up with a rusty squealing of its brakes in front of the little station, looking pretty much exhausted after its tough climb into town. The engineer piled out of the cab, grease-marked outside and full of hard feelings and frustrations inside. He began to work on the old locomotive, squirting grease here and there into its aged joints.

I looked down the track and there spilling out of the Jim Crow car—as always there were only four cars, a white car, a Negro car, a freight car, and a caboose—came a swarm of little Negro school girls all dressed in their pink and white and blue holiday garments and with ribbons in their hair, and also a sprinkling of young Negro boys, all ironed and pressed and scrubbed clean by their mamas for this occasion. In the lead of the young people was a tall yellow Negro man wearing gold-rimmed glasses, a flat-topped straw hat, and with a wide expanse of white stiff-starched shirt front showing, topped off by a wing collar and a big black bolster tie. The little Negro children twittered and chirped in the sunny air, looking happily about them. I wondered where they were going, and then I heard the Confederate veteran say that they were on a "skursion" to Durham no doubt. Evidently this was the ending of the school year and the teacher was celebrating by taking his students to Durham. The big yellow man came strolling forward toward the station and toward the irate and sweating engineer. I could see he felt good, the world was sitting to his hand.

"Good morning, gentlemen," he said with a smile, and his glance swept by, including me, and I was proud that he had noticed me. The old Confederate soldier blinked up at him and continued leaning on his stick, saying nothing. I naturally said nothing, but I was already in my heart admiring this big and successful member of the Negro race.

"What time do the train get to Durham, sir?" the Negro asked of the engineer.

"None of your damned business!" the engineer snapped instantly back, still bent over one of the drivers with his oil can. Then he looked around and straightened himself spasmodically up, glaring at the colored man.

The Negro had taken a rebuffed step backward.

"Sorry, sir, sorry," he said, and his head began bobbing up and down a bit, his body bending at the waist.

"Take off your hat!" the engineer suddenly shouted. And my hand started instinctively up to my own cap to pull it off and then dropped as I saw the hat of the Negro teacher come quickly off. The little children down at the other end of the train sensed something was beginning to be wrong and were already twittering and huddling together as if a threat were being felt in the air. And it was. I felt it.

"Take off them specs too!" the engineer snarled as he stood up. "Ain't no place for a biggity nigger here."

"But I ain't done nothing, white folks, ain't done a thing," said the colored teacher, and he backed away a couple of steps more. I, not knowing it till I later remembered it, backed away with him.

"Don't white-folks me!" the engineer squealed.

Then he flung the oil can behind him, snatched the walking stick from under the Confederate soldier's resting hand and quick as lightning turned and struck the Negro teacher a terrific blow across the face. I shut my eyes with a choking gasp. And like in a sunlit mirror I suddenly could see in my mind that the stick was splintered in the middle and already stained with blood.

A little babble of shrieks and moanings rose from the school children there in the distance. I opened my eyes, but only halfway, and peered out, and I saw that the children were bounding up the steps of the Jim Crow car and inside for safety like a gang of terrified goats. And I noticed too that the Confederate soldier had almost fallen on his face when his support was jerked away, but now was righting himself with spread-out legs, and the engineer was handing his walking stick back to him and he was resuming his resting on it without a word. I couldn't look at the stick. I couldn't look at the Negro teacher. I shivered and shook as if some freezing rain and pall of darkness were spreading over the world. I heard a piteous whining sound coming from the Negro schoolteacher, and then I heard him say quietly, "White folks, you done ruint my shirt."

"All aboard!" the engineer yelled. And climbing hastily into his cab, he pulled the whistle-cord a couple of times, and the old locomotive gave out a fearful hoarse shrieking. The Negro schoolteacher turned away, still holding his big white handkerchief, now dyeing a crimson red, against his face and above his blood-spattered shirt front.

And I turned and fled down the railroad track toward the boxcar where my father and the wagon were waiting. And in me was a dreadful grief and wild lament to the earth and sky.

"Oh, oh, can't somebody do something—do something to help!" my heart was crying. "Oh! oh! oh! Help! Help!"

Uncle Reuben and the Ku Klux Klan

One day when I was about twelve years old I was out in the field working with Uncle Reuben Bailey, the old Negro cradler. He was cutting our spring oats and I was manfully following, tying them in bundles behind him as best I could. The day was hot, and along about the middle of the morning we went over to the apple tree in the edge of the field where our water was. After I had drunk from the jug first (me being white), the old Negro lifted the jug to his lips. As he tilted it back I watched the water wads go gluk-gluk down his wrinkled old throat—a throat as black and scaly as the hide of that alligator I had seen in the circus at Dunn. And then I noticed another thing. The sleeve of his ragged homemade shirt slipped back and there were two round whitish spots showing on his forearm.

He set the jug down, reached back in the shade, fanned himself a bit more and pulled out a piece of his petrified rock and began sharpening the cradle blade. And once more his old sleeve slipped back up his forearm from his lifted hand and there were those spots again. I happened to notice them, idly at first. And then I stared at them. He saw I was looking at his arm. He pushed the cradle from him and slid the whetstone back into his pocket.

"You notice things, don't you?" he said.

"I dunno, Uncle Reuben," I answered uncertainly.

"Yeh, you do. You got sharp eyes. I notice that 'bout a lot of things. And now you done crossed the line of accountability, ain't you?"

" 'Countability? Yes, the preachers say I have."

"So I reckon whilst we set and blow a little I mought as well tell you about them spots you been looking at, now that you got so far in the world. I notice you keep looking at 'em."

"Yeh, I bet you've had bad carbuncles like that peddler had."

"Sump'n worse'n carbuncles," he said with a chuckle.

"What? What was that?"

"Hot lead, boy," he answered abruptly, "bullet lead."

"Bullets?"

"That's what I say. That's where I was shot 'way back in the Ku Klux times—right after the Civil War."

I knew about the Ku Klux of course and how they had gone about frightening Negroes soon after slavery was ended. And now I remembered hearing that Uncle Reuben as a young man had been mixed up in some kind of trouble, some kind of killing. But I had never heard the story. Nobody would talk about it. My father wouldn't. And now at last I was going to hear all about it. I squirmed up a bit closer.

"Did the Ku Klux shoot you?" I asked eagerly.

"Yeah, one of them Ku Klux did."

"Who was it, Uncle Reuben?"

"Now you know good and well I ain't going to tell you 'bout no particular person. It was just the Ku Klux shot me. I'll show you sump'n else." And pushing up to his feet, he undid his homemade britches, pulled up his shirt and showed me another spot on his side. And then he turned around and shamelessly dropped his trousers farther down, disclosing another mark low on his stringy, seamed stern. "Yes, suh, son," he went on, "that's where them bullets hit me." He stuck his shirt in and buttoned his britches again. "They sho' poured the lead into me that time."

I sat there staring at him horrified—yet thrilled too. I was all in a shivering tumult to hear more.

"How did it happen? How did it, Uncle Reuben?" I said.

He went on. "The niggers had been cutting up too brief, I reckon, after they got their freedom, me amongst 'em. Well, so they come waiting on me. When I heard the Ku Kluxers outside my door I told 'em not to come in 'cause I was right inside there and I had my axe handy. 'Don't come in here,' I said. 'I'll kill the first man breaks in my door!' But that didn't stop 'em. They whoomed and lunged against the door and they broke it down. And the first man that tumbled in was Mr. Ed Gasking, and what did I do with my axe but split him clean down to the belly-button. Lord, lord, I split him on down."

And then I remembered too that I had heard something about a Mr. Gaskins that got killed long, long ago in the Ku Klux trouble. Speechless, I gazed at Uncle Reuben. And he was no longer just Uncle Reuben but a man with something suddenly mysterious and strange about him. He had killed somebody.

He chuckled again and dug into the ground with one of his long-nailed bony fingers. "Course I been sorry for that a long, long time. I been sorry. But I been done forgive for it by the old Master up there," and he gestured toward the sky. Then a medley of little whickering chuckles broke from him as he spat a spurt of brown tobacco juice off to one side. "But tough, I was tough! They poured the lead into me and mowed me down, but they couldn't kill this nigger, no sir! And there I was lying on that floor that night and that Ku Klux man standing over me with the smoking pistol in his hand and the other dead body lying there all split open, bleeding on the floor. Well, I could see that man against the door light and I could smell the powder in the room too, even smell the fresh blood. I still had my good senses about me. And you know what that Ku Klux with the pistol said while he was standing over me?"

"No, I don't," I spoke up breathlessly.

"He said, 'I reckon that's done for you, you damn black scoundrel. But I'll make sho' of it.' And he bent over in the dark and he fired that last bullet smack at me. He'd already shot me five times. And that made six. But maybe in the dark his hand was too trembly, so he just grazed the side of my skelp here." And Uncle Reuben lifted his old black hat back, pushed up a bit of his kinky white hair and there sure enough just along the side above his ear was a slick hairless mark.

"Lord," I breathed, "Lord!"

"Yeh, they shot me down like a dog," he went on easily, even pridefully. "Maybe I was deserving of it some. I was a young buck then and I had just got my freedom, as I say. Maybe I was shooting off my mouth round and about a little too much. And that's how come they come waiting on me in the deep dead of night, them Ku Kluxers. Yes."

"Did you know who it was shot you, Uncle Reuben? Who?"

"Sure I knowed him. He pulled off his old sheet headgear and he looked down at me laying on the floor that night. I seen him clear. I would've knowed his voice anyhow, 'cause him and me had worked in the fields together many a time, in fact—ah—yeah, many a time."

"Who was it?"

"Now behave yourself. You know I ain't gonna tell you that."

"After that what happened? What happened?"

"Well, they carried the dead man off from there, away from my house, and later I crawled out through the door and across the fields and got into a ditch. And I lay in that ditch all that night and the next day, and that's where Nedgelena, the gal I later married, found me. And she and her mammy pulled and toted me off in the dark to their cabin and they hid me in the smokehouse and treated me with salt poultices and axle grease and turpentine salve till I got well."

"And then what, Uncle Reuben?"

"Well, I laid mighty low, hid out, as I say and am here to tell you. And by the time I got well the feeling had sort of blowed over. People had learnt better. But I moved off to Sampson County anyhow and farmed there for a few years, then come back here on your daddy's land, and I been here ever since. Yes sir, people were riled up back in them days and all on account of us niggers—Lord help my life, what do I see yonder." And he sprang to his feet quick as a young man. I turned my head and then I jumped up too, for there coming across the field all dressed out in his white linen suit and Panama hat and swinging his gold-headed cane in the summer sun was my Uncle Heck. Both Uncle Reuben and I had been so intent on the Ku Klux story that we hadn't heard the sound of the buggy or the trotting horse coming up the lane. A letter had come in the mail the day before to my father saying he, Uncle Heck, was coming up from Wilmington, where he was postmaster, to visit us. Uncle Reuben now quickly spat out his tobacco juice, cleared his throat, spat again, wiped his face, gave his kinky hair a rake with his long fingers, and finished buttoning his trousers—primping himself.

"How you there, Reuben?" Uncle Heck called, stepping along toward us. And already Uncle Reuben was grinning and bowing up and down, his hat in his hand while he answered back.

"Bless the Lord, there you is, Mr. Heck—a sight for sore eyes. Yes sir, glory be to the Lord on high!" And he scrambled out to meet Uncle Heck. And I stood there, a little twelve-year-old, sweat-sodden fool, watching those two older fools. For as they met there in the middle of the lone oat field—Uncle Heck with his fine summer clothes and his gray clean-cut military mustache and gold-rimmed eyeglasses and Panama hat and cane, a gentleman great and airy, and Uncle Reuben smelly and dust-begrimed and a Negro at that—Uncle Heck threw his arms around him and hugged him and Uncle Reuben hugged him back. Without hardly knowing what I did I picked up the water jug and went nearer to them.

"Well, you old black scoundrel, you ain't aged a day since last year," said Uncle Heck.

"And you, Mr. Heck, you look like sump'n stepped out of the bandbox of heaven, always a spick-and-span gentleman." And Uncle Reuben peered at him. "One thing I miss though," he said, "that purty flower you allus wears in your button hole."

"Well, I've stopped that, Reuben, stopped it," Uncle Heck laughed. "The gay girls in town have quit smiling at me since I'm so old, so I said to myself, 'What use is there in buying a gardenia anymore?' You keeping well, Reuben?"

"Yes suh, yes suh, tip top."

And then Uncle Heck looked out at me and gestured with his fabulous cane. "Hi, Paul son, how you doing, boy? I reckon you're Paul. My goodness, you've grown!"

"All right, Uncle Heck," I stammered, my head swimming with joy. Lord, I loved that man!

"Is he smart to work, Reuben?" Uncle Heck queried.

"Yes, he do the best he kin," Uncle Reuben chuckled. "But stories—that's what he likes best—stories. He's lately all the time after me about things—about darky songs, whether I done seen a ha'nt or not, old folks tales, that stuff."

"Yes, I remember him well enough. Always pestering me to tell him about the war."

"Yessuh, that's him," said Uncle Reuben.

"Well, if he wants to hear a real tale, you ought to tell him about the Ku Klux times, Reuben."

"Yes, sir, I told him something about that, seeing's how manhood is about to come on him and he done crossed the line of 'countability."

Uncle Heck turned to me. "So Reuben told you about the Ku Klux?"

"Yes sir," I answered.

"Did he tell you about poor Ed Gaskins?"

"Yes sir," I gulped, "the one that got killed with the axe."

"And what else?" And Uncle Heck was staring sharply yet smilingly at me now.

"That's all, Mr. Heck," said Uncle Reuben. "That's all."

"And a Ku Kluxer shot Uncle Reuben down in the floor," I added.

"That's right, that's right," said Uncle Heck. "And did Reuben tell you who the Ku Kluxer was?"

"Now Mr. Heck, you know I know better'n that," Uncle Reuben broke in.

"No sir, he didn't."

"Tell him, Reuben," and he laughed. "He and his line of accountability. That would be a story to last him for a while."

But Reuben shook his head. "Lord, no sir," he said.

And then Uncle Heck pushed the end of his cane at Reuben and laughed again. "You know what today is, Reuben?" he said.

"No sir."

"It's an anniversary. It's the sixth of May." Then he looked over at me. "Forty-two years ago it was, son, when he was shot. Walking along downtown Saturday I thought of it. And in honor of that occasion, Reuben, I brought you a whole box full of Brown Mule tobacco, there in the buggy." And he gestured off toward the house.

"The Lord bless you, bless you from his heavenly bosom!" said Uncle Reuben. And he grabbed Uncle Heck's hand and held it and kissed it. And Uncle Heck laughed again and called out to me, as he winked his eye all merry like.

"Look here, Paul, son," he said. "Look, you see Reuben kissing my hand. Well, this is the very hand that shot him down one night forty-two years ago."

I dropped the water jug with a bump.

Now the bell in the yard of our little house across the field began to ring for mealtime, and Uncle Reuben and Uncle Heck turned and moved on across the field, and forgetting the water jug, I followed. And there they were walking in the summer weather ahead of me. Uncle Heck's arm was around Uncle Reuben's shoulders, and they both were laughing and talking over the old days, cronies, bosom buddies in these latter days. Ah, Lord!

Nicholas and Second Sight

One day when a group of us local historians visited Old Long Street Church, now on the Fort Bragg Military Reservation, Mr. Shaw, one of the members, told us at that time about a Negro man named Nicholas who had this gift of second sight.

"Over across the creek there," said Mr. Shaw, "a family lived, consisting of a mother and daughter, six sons and the father. Well, in the Civil War the father and sons went away to fight, and they were all killed. But before the news came that they were killed Nicholas had a vision of the killing. This Nicholas was a runaway slave just passing through the neighborhood, and he came to the house over there and asked the good lady if she could feed him and give him a place to sleep in the barn. He looked like an honest fellow and she being lonesome with her husband and six sons gone to war said he could. My daddy told me about this.

"Well, the next morning Nicholas came to the house, his hat in his hand, and he said, 'Missus, the Lord's done come to me in a vision last night, and the Lord said to me, "Nicholas," he said, "the good lady's husband and six sons has been killed." And then the husband, your good man, he appeared to me in a dream. I saw him in second sight clear as the pa'm of my hand, and he said to me, he said, "Nicholas, me and my boys have all been done killed and I want you to keep on staying there with my wife to take care of things.

I want you to do that, Nicholas." And I said to him, "Cap'n," I said, "I'll sure do it." '

"So it was that Nicholas stayed there the rest of his life," said Mr. Shaw, "and looked after the mother and the daughter, for his second-sight seeing was true.

"Well, time went on, the years passed by, changes came. The mother and the daughter they died and only Nicholas was left alive. He was an old man by this time and he stayed in the house that had belonged to the good lady, for the daughter had left it to him. He lived there until the time the government took over the reservation here in 1923.

"Some of you know what a hard time the government had in getting folks to give up their land here at Fort Bragg. But finally after a lot of hard trials everybody had been taken care of except Nicholas. He refused to budge. The authorities had to get the law of course and at last they put him out, they evicted him. They moved him and his goods down the road there.

"What do you think—the very next day Nicholas was back in the same house. They moved him out again. He came back again.

"Finally my daddy and General Bowley came out here to see Nicholas. The General got interested in him, and my daddy told him the story of Nicholas, the way I'm telling it. I think the General was touched by it. Anyhow, he said, 'Nicholas, you stay right here. You can stay on as long as you want to. Of course, we've got an artillery range here but we'll take care of you somehow.'

"So every time after that before they'd start the artillery practice, they'd first send a soldier or soldiers over to tell Nicholas that they were about ready to fire and Nicholas would move out of there. And where do you think he'd come? He'd come here to this old Longstreet Church and wait here till the firing was over.

"Of course by that time the church was long deserted, the congregation had passed on and there was no service held here at all. But Nicholas would come here, sit down in the church, and wait until the thunder and fire of the artillery was over just down there to the south of us.

"I reckon a lot of us wonder what the old colored man thought about as he sat here in this church and heard the roar of the guns.

"Yes, he was the last worshiper in Longstreet Church," said Mr. Shaw, "and now nothing ever comes here much except a lot of deer that take shelter from the cold weather under the building."

Later I went out and looked under the church. The north end was some five and a half feet from the ground which sloped upward to a couple of feet at the rear. The earth was covered with deer manure. "Enough," said Leon MacDonald, one of the historians, "to make my garden rich as sin."

Big John

There are many tales told about Big John and his gluttony and laziness, and I have heard them from different sources. I copied down one Aunt Fanny McDade told me about the old rapscallion. Aunt Fanny was a prideful Negro who owned her own home in Chapel Hill, at the corner of Cameron Avenue and Graham Street, and lived to be a hundred and four years old. She died in 1964. She used to say to her friends with a chuckle, "I come in with Lincoln but I didn't go out with him." She was for a long time a favorite with the university people and her recollections went far back to Mrs. Spencer, Presidents Battle, Winston, and others and on up to recent days. I copied down many of the things she told me about Chapel Hill, and in one of my notebooks I wrote down her story of Big John.

"Yessuh, yessuh, Mr. Green," she said one day as she lifted her heavy sadiron off the lacy dress she was ironing for one of the university wives and peering over her steel-rimmed spectacles at me, "put this tight in your noggin. There are plenty of people in this world who holler Lord and follow devil. And they make a lot of squeal and little wool as this same old Satan said when he sheared his hogs. And Big John was like that, a hypocrite from way back, in the old days. Yessuh, he was a lazy and good-for-nothing old scoundrel, that's what he was. And there was nothing he liked better than to lie up and snooze whilst his wife and children did all the hard work. And there in his bed he kept saying and pretending he was sicker'n he was and that he wouldn't be long for this world and soon would be flapping his wings at the pearly gates. And he had one speech which he kept calling out—'Old Moster in Heaven, come down quick and take me, take me whole soul and body, away to thy mansion in the skies.' And that's the kind of tune he kept a-going.

"And people passing along the road, the neighbors, could hear this old nigger lying up there in his featherbed a-praying and a-talking this good holy talk. And the folks brought him plenty of good things to eat, seeing as how he was so close to God they thought. But it was all a blind. For that old devil wasn't any more interested in religion than a goat in a diadem. As I said, it was just his excuse to laze and do nothing and eat the good things his wife and children worked out for him and the neighbors brought in.

"It may be easy to fool the niggers, Mr. Green, but you take it from me, you can't fool the good white folks, not for long. They've got brains—even like you and the other 'fessors that teach in the university here. So it was that good old Moster Landlord, the white man, was on to old Big John. He could see through him. So he said to Big John's wife one day, he said, 'Liza'—her name was Liza—'you and me's got to do something 'bout him.'

" 'Yes sir, Marse Landlord,' said Liza.

"And so they put their heads together in a manner of speaking and made their plans.

"Now one day in the fall when the cotton was hanging white as snow in the field and needed picking mighty bad, ole Big John was lying up in the bed there same as usual and putting out his prayers and hollers more than ever. You see he was slick, the worse the cotton needed picking, the louder was his holy talk. And he was sending forth his refrain, 'Do Lord God, old Moster, Savior mine, come and get me, whole soul and body! Come now, I'm in a state of grace and pure and ready.'

"And then right spang in the middle of the night and in his praying and his talking there come a heavy tromp, tromp on the porch and a bam, bam, bam on the side of the weatherboarding and then a big gross voice calling out, 'All right, Big John, here I am, I've come for you.'

"Old Big John didn't quite catch the words at first. And so he prayed out louder than ever. 'O Heavenly Father,' he said, 'take me, Father, to thy holy sweet-resting bosom, crown me with thy spangs of glory, fit me with a garment of joy and let me circle the battlements of Heaven like a pigeon white as snow and the sun shining on me making my whings' —he said 'whings'—'yea, let me, Heavenly Father, sing thy praises celestial evermore.'

"Yes, just like that was the way I heard it.

"And now the voice out on the porch boomed out good and loud, so loud that Big John couldn't help hearing it. 'All right, Big John, your prayers are answered. I've come to get you forevermore.' Old Big John listened and then shivered and shook and made the bed slats rattle with his trembling.

" 'Who's that, who's that?' he said.

" 'It's me, the Great Lord God of Heaven and I've come for you in answer to your prayers—whole soul and body.'

"Old Big John he still shivered and shook but he quavered out in a little small voice, 'Thank you, God.'

" 'Make haste,' said the great voice, 'I've got no time to spare. This is a busy day. I'm gathering in the souls sanctified all round and about. And several big sinners are waiting there beyonst Haywood town.'

"And old Big John lying there in the bed did some mighty quick thinking. He raised up in his nightshirt and slid his feet out on the floor and sat there scratching his head and finally he said in a humble sweet voice, 'Oh, Big Moster God, please suh, open the do' so I can look out over my crop and say goodbye to it, suh. I wants to say goodbye to all these earthly scenes below,' he said. So the white Marse Landlord standing out of sight on the porch in the darkness pulled back the door a little bit.

" 'C'mon, Big John,' he said, 'make it in a hurry.'

" 'Yes suh,' said Big John, now a little more cheerful-like. 'Just gimme time, suh, to get my hat. It might be mighty cold flying up to heaven through them icy stars. And you wouldn't want me to ketch cold, would you, Marse God?'

" 'That's right, I wouldn't. Get your coat too,' said the white landlord.

" 'And please, suh, could you crack the do' a little mo' furder so I can get a last look at the barn where my Mary mule is resting? It's mighty sad to say goodbye to that faithful mule and me plowing her so many days and hard.'

"And Marse Landlord pulled the door open a little wider. And with that old Big John set hisself, and out he went, same as if the hounds of the Bad Place were after him. And all in his nightshirt he flew and with his derby hat set 'pon top of his head.

"Now the wife and children were standing out in the yard. They were on to the trick played by Marse White Landlord, and so Liza she screamed out, 'Run, John, run!'

"And the children they screamed out, 'Run, Pappy, run!' And by this time Marse White Landlord with his white sheet on was chasing John in a hurry 'cross the cotton patch. And Liza screamed out again, 'Run, John, run, God's a-gaining on you!'

"And, Mr. Green! John showered down on his speed and he left God behind him same as if Jehovah was mired down in deep mud up to his knees. Yessir, old John's feet that night were shod with the wind, they say. And the pocket of his nightshirt dipped sand, they tell it, as he turned the edge of the field and was gone from there through the woods. And to say you the truth, that nigger wasn't seen in the neighborhood for weeks on end. Then one day he come walking back over the hill and he was wearing shoes and a shirt and working overalls. And guess what he had in his hands. Guess. Why, he had a maul and a wedge, a maul and a wedge to work in his new ground. And he set to work and they said he was a mighty man at splitting cordwood and getting up grubs from then on, for you see, God had ketched him and put that maul and wedge in his hand.

"God ketches everybody. 'Member that, son. Remember."

"Yes, Aunt Fanny, I'll remember."

Folk Medicine

I remember being in Hood and Grantham's Drug Store in the town of Dunn once, and discussing with Mr. Grantham, who happened to be a trustee of the University where I taught, the huge display of patent medicine he had on his shelves—Dr. Pierce's Golden Remedy Discoveries, Sarsaparilla, Cardui, Lydia Pinkham's Vegetable Compound, Peruna, Carter's Little Liver Pills, etc., etc., and he told me that he eased his conscience in selling the stuff through the fact that so many people got cured or helped by it, because they believed in it. For instance, he says, "Take Peruna, I sell hundreds of bottles of that stuff and, of course, a lot of our prohibition guys who can't get liquor drink it for its kick. But patent medicine is here to stay," he said.

While we were talking, a Negro woman came in with a little boy. She called Mr. Grantham "Doctor." "Doctor," she said, "I brung the boy here for you to look at him like you said."

Mr. Grantham took the boy and, followed by the woman, went into the rear of the store. I heard him back there saying a few things, and then pretty soon he came out and got a little tin box of salve from a shelf and sold it to the woman for fifty cents which she fished deep out of her knotted handkerchief, and she and the boy went outside. Mr. Grantham continued, "Take that boy there, now he's got what you call a dropped palate, and his mother brought him in here two or three days ago. I tried to get her to go to the doctor, but she didn't believe in the regular doctors. She said that I must have some kind of medicine here to help her boy, and she asked me to work on him. And so back there a moment ago I took a bit of his kinky wool, got hold of it on top of his head, gave it two or three jerks, and looked in his mouth and told him that his palate was getting all right, and then I sold her this salve to rub on his throat."

I stared at Mr. Grantham in shocked surprise. He shrugged his shoulders, laughed, and said, "Human nature's funny, ain't it?" I nodded and started out of the store, and then stopped, "That reminds me," I said, "I wanted a bottle, large size, of Vick's nosedrops."

"Coming right up," said Mr. Grantham, as he turned to the shelf with a chuckle.

Then there was the case of Dr. Hyde. One day I was sitting with Mr. Mac in his millhouse, eating a barbecue lunch snack, and he told me that perhaps the most famous fake doctor of the old days in the Valley was this Dr. Hyde.

"Now you may know," he said, "that back in the old times people in the Valley believed more in healing by prayer and laying on of consecrated hands than they do now, though you might not think so, seeing the doings at Falcon and in so many of the Pentecostal Holiness Churches round and about. But they did, at least I think so. Anyway the story of Dr. Hyde would seem to prove it.

"Well, during a long protracted meeting at old Moriah Church all sorts of people with aches and pains came in to be healed, by prayer and laying on of hands. And the Holy Ghost, they say, was powerful in their behalf. Right in the midst of things, though, this Doctor Hyde showed up trying to sell his folk medicines. But the Holy Spirit had been doing so well with the sick and infirm that business for him was no good at all, that is, at first.

"Hyde had a light wagon fixed up like a peddler's outfit. And on each side of the wagon body he had painted in big letters 'DOCTOR HYDE'S HOME REMEDIES.' He had a little Negro boy that drove for him, all dressed up like a monkey with a red cap and a coat with bells on it. And remedies! Dr. Hyde had them. He had a madstone cure for snake bite and rabies, wart cures, pills for chills and fever, tonics for rundown feelings and lost manhood, cures for boils, tetters, scurvy, scrofula, dropsy, piles, fistula, gravel, female obstructions, nightmares, purges for bile and yellow ja'ndice, and powders for dysentery, liver complaint, and salivation—everything you could think of. He even had a yellow turpentine salve for the cure of the seven-year itch, bone felons, and syphilis.

"So this 'doctor' drove around from door to door in the neighborhood but he sold nothing. Next day when the revival meeting was in full swing at the church he showed up there. The little Negro sat outside while the doctor went in. The testimonies were going on, and different people were standing up one by one to give thanks unto Jesus and Him crucified and bespeaking the list of their bountiful blessings. When he got a chance Doctor Hyde stood up. He too humbly thanked the Lord for all his tender mercy. This time he said he was especially thankful for the privilege God had given him in helping to cure the misery of the wide and suffering world. He went on and told something then about his medicines. God had called him to be a doctor, he said. And God told him what to fix to cure folks. Yessir and amen, God had watched over him and instructed him in the healing herbs and mystic mixtures.

"Well, that warmed 'em up a little more. And the next day he got so far as to go around in the congregation and talk to the sinners with the rest of the deacons and holy sisters. And after Aunt Sudie Horton had brought up her dozen sanctified handkerchiefs to be put on the sore and afflicted, Dr. Hyde rose and said he wanted the sisters and brothers to pray over his medicines so they might be increased in the power of their healing too, like the blessed handkerchiefs.

"After the church broke up they all went out to his wagon and stood around with their hands on it and consecrated it to the glory of God and the uplift of man. That made him one of them. And a number of folks bought some of his stuff. He told them he hated to charge them for it, and all it cost them was what it cost him. The government made him pay to bring the original ingredient stuff into this country, else he'd give it away free. He said he got the height of it from somewhere away in Asia or Africa.

"Then lo and behold, the next day at church he about took charge of the meeting. He stood up and praised God and slapped his hands and said he'd just got news from Virginia where two blind people had been cured with his medicines, and another one was cured of stuttering and was planning to become a preacher. Amen. And he went on telling of this and that, what he had done and what he could do. Everything, he said, was by the grace of God. Nothing in his own strength. When he spoke about the blind folks everybody thought of Em Lucas and her bastard children—every one of them blind and Em herself blind. Everybody knew it was some bad blood disease made it, old rale or something. But they all had got to believing in him so by this time that they hoped he could do something for Em and her young ones. So some of the freehearted bought several bottles of this rain water and took it down to Em. David Vance and Green Mumford, two unregenerate sinners who had lasted out the meeting, chipped in about half of the price. They said they didn't believe in it but still you never could tell. They too had felt the persuasion of Dr. Hyde no doubt. That day Dr. Hyde did a rushing business. It was the last day of the meeting and he made it count. But he wasn't satisfied. The next day was to be the big baptizing at the Williams's millpond. And he announced that he was going to prove his loving devotion to his God by working a miracle. He wanted everybody to pray for him that it might be so. Jesus walked on the sea of Galilee, he said, and if the spirit was with him he might try the same in Williams's millpond.

"He showed up with his wagon loaded down with remedies. No doubt he and that little Negro had worked part of the night down at the creek by lantern light coloring water, filling up bottles, and sticking on labels. Another part of the night they had been busy at something else, as David Vance and Green Mumford found out.

"Dave and Green were coming along home about three o'clock in the morning from sparking some gals over by Barclaysville. The weather was hot and the two rounders had been drinking mighty freely of Jamaica rum and needed to cool off. So they stopped when they got to the millpond and went in swimming, muddy as it was. And in paddling around they bumped into a narrow plank walkway built somewhat under the water. At first they didn't know what in the dickens it was, for foot planks usually went over the water, not in it or under it. Then by putting two and two together they concluded that it was part of Dr. Hyde's doing and was connected with his miracle for the baptizing. The old rapscallion and the Negro had been there earlier in the night and put it up. So Dave and Green to surprise the doctor quietly lifted out a long section of the planking and carried it off.

"Dr. Hyde came next day with mergins of medicines. He told the folks he'd been to the Cape Fear siding where a fresh new supply had just been shipped in from the old world. He got the preachers and deacons to give him a little time before the ducking begun. He stood up in his wagon and soon had the whole crowd around him. And there was a crowd there that day, everybody for miles and their neighbors, it seemed like. Such a roll of talk as he turned loose! And all the time that little Negro sat there without saying a word. He was on to it all and he must have been snickering in his sleeve at the gang of fools handing up their dimes and dollars. Dr. Hyde did a business that was a business that day. Lord he was a greedy man! He wasn't satisfied. When he'd sold out, he told the folks that he fully believed God had given him power to work miracles.

"And while the Negro boy drove off to get another load of his mess that he had hid somewhere in a fence jamb, he announced to the crowd that through the strength of his medicine and the power of God he was now going to try to walk on water. By this time he had just about everybody hypnotized. Blest if he didn't tear loose into the water, right spank! He fluttered and floundered about a minute and then stood up with his hands crossed in front of him and praying and carrying on like he was talking straight to God. And he walked right on off where the water was about ten feet deep. And it didn't come up much above calf-leg high. The folks fell down on their knees and shouted and cut up, same as if the Savior had come back. In a minute the doctor was back on the bank and when he struck dry ground he struck it singing—singing the old hymn about "power, power, wonder-working power." I don't know how many fresh converts were made. But I know Dave Vance and Green Mumford weren't among them. They stood on the outside of the crowd looking on, waiting. By this time the little Negro was back with a load of bottles, and the doctor started haranguing the crowd again. But sales were slowing down now. No doubt the old glutton had got about all the money present, but he still wasn't satisfied. So he announced he would walk on water even farther, and for everybody to believe in the power of himself and his medicine sanctified. So he hauled off and made another floundering out in the water, got set and walked as before except farther. And that's where he hung himself.

"For while the people looked on, all overpowered with awe, the doctor came to the pitfall prepared for him, even as the scriptures say, except this time it was dug in the water. And down he went like a rock kerchoog and out of sight. Well, to sum the thing up in a word, the old hypocrite nigh drowned before it occurred to anybody to jump in to save him. For he couldn't swim a lick. Then several of the brothers dived in after him, while the women screamed. But not Dave Vance and Green Mumford. They were a stony-hearted pair all right, and they kept whooming about and laughing out loud. And then the folks found the footlog contraption, and so exposed the doctor.

"It looked for a while as if the people would lynch the old devil when they found out the trick he'd played. Dave and Green helped protect him from the wrath of the crowd, but in spite of them he got his britches torn off of him, and his money with them. And he was whipped black and blue before he got loose and struck a lope toward the mountains to the west. The little Negro had already bolted—when he saw his master sink under the water.

"And neither one of them was ever seen in Little Bethel from that day to this. The folks gave the money and the horse and wagon to poor blind Em Lucas. That helped her some. The medicine didn't."

The School-Breaking

As a child I attended Old Pleasant Union School located about halfway between Lillington and Angier on a rather direct line. It was a one-room building and was heated by a huge fireplace. We boys playing horsey used to go into the woods and drag eight-foot-length dead logs in at the front door and across the floor and roll them into the huge fireplace. I don't remember that we ever had any school-breaking exercises in this one-room building. But later my father and the neighbors got together, tore down the old one-room cabin, and put up a nice frame two-room building. We always referred to these rooms as the big room and the little room. A sliding partition was put up between these rooms, and I remember that some of us boys working low down near the floor cut a hole through the partition and used to pass love notes through to some of the girls we were sweet on.

After we were provided with this two-room schoolhouse we began to have school-breaking exercises in the spring on the day school ended. These exercises usually consisted of little bits of poetry, recitations, and even sometimes a bit of a play scene. I remember one playlet we put on which had to do with a stupid Negro boy who takes some of the white folks' clothes off to be laundered with the understanding that he is to "mangle" them. I played the Negro boy, and when I brought the clothes back all mangled, I got a big hand from the audience. Maybe this little playlet had something to do with my later writing so many Negro dramas. One of the exercises I always loved at the school-breaking time was the liars' contest. Two boys would come out on the little stage and engage each other in as wild imagery of outdoing as possible. The material in most of these liars' contests was provided by the boys themselves.

I remember the last school-breaking I ever attended at Pleasant Union. The next year I went to school at Buies Creek Academy. Baxter Upchurch and I tried to outdo each other in lying. We came out on the little stage, simulating two neighbors meeting on a road. We started off with some of the Arkansas Traveler dialogue. I said to Baxter, "Hello, stranger."

And he replied, "Hell-o yourself—if you want to go to hell, then go there yourself."

Paul (looking about him): Why don't you cover your house here? (I gesture toward the unseen house.)

Baxter: Can't cover it when it's raining and when it's dry, it don't leak a drop.

Paul (Gazing around again): What makes your corn look so yellow?

Baxter: Fool, I planted the yellow kind.

Paul: Um-um. How did your 'taters turn out?

Baxter: Didn't turn out, fool, I dug 'em out.

Paul: Say, tell me how far is it to where the road forks.

Baxter: Been living here fifty years and it ain't forked yet.

Paul: Reckon I can ford the river?

Baxter: Reckon so, any goose can.

Paul: Say, yonder comes a steer. You better head him.

Baxter: I gad, looks like he's got a head on him.

Paul: I mean stop him.

Baxter: Ain't got no stopper.

Paul: I mean turn him.

Baxter: Don't need no turning, he's already got the hairy side out.

Paul: Well, well, well. Say, have you lived here all your life?

Baxter: Not all of it, fool, for I ain't dead yet.

Paul: Goodness alive! You don't answer anything—you sure are ignorant!

Baxter: I know I ain't lost like you. Ha, ha, ha! (And then we would change the subject and get on with our whoppers.)

Paul: I haven't seen you much lately, Baxter.

Baxter: No, I've been mighty busy.

Paul: What you been doing?

Baxter: Clearing my new ground.

Paul: How do you clear your new ground, Baxter?

Baxter: Well, I go into the middle of the woods, find a big tree, get plenty of sticks of dynamite, fasten them around the tree, and set 'em off, and the explosion clears me several acres all at once.

Paul: And what happens to you?

Baxter: Why, I just grab a tree and ride out. Ha, ha, ha!

Paul: Well, I've been pretty busy myself, Baxter.

Baxter: What have you been doing, Paul?

Paul: Looking after my watermelons. Lord, Lord, and how they do grow!

Baxter: They do?

Paul: Yeh, do. I've been busy making little low platforms with wheels to 'em.

Baxter: What in the name of old Scratch you doing that for?

Paul: Because my land is so rich and the watermelon vines grow so fast that they drag the watermelons along the ground and wear them out, so I put these little wagons under the melons so they won't be dragged to death, and the vines drag the little wagons along with the melons on them and they grow bigger and bigger all the time.

Baxter: How big they grow?

Paul: Oh, a certain size. Sometimes the wagons run into the fence and stop and the watermelons grow right there bigger and bigger, and you can look out and see the tops of them, the tops of the rinds over the fence.

Baxter: Um-um—your melons are almost big as my cabbages.

Paul: And how big are they, Baxter?

Baxter: Oh, pretty big. I lost my sow and pigs the other day and hunted them and hunted them, and finally I found them. The old sow had et a hole way back in one of my cabbages and there she was as snug as you please, her and the twelve pigs, all shoat size.

Paul: Well, well, well.

Baxter: And I've been raising some chickens lately too. I got a rooster can eat two of them cabbages in one bait.

Paul: Ah, that rooster's a little biddy compared to my turkey. I got a gobbler that is a gobbler.

Baxter: How big is your gobbler, Paul?

Paul: Well, he's so big he can set a-straddle the Pacific Ocean, and pick stars out of the elements for grains of corn. Ha, ha, ha!

Baxter: Well, that is a pretty big gobbler, a little bigger than the catfish my Uncle Zacharias caught in the Cape Fear River last year, I'll have to agree. That fish was so big we had to get four teams of mules and a log wagon to drag him up the bank. And when we cut him open with the axe and a crosscut saw, we found six cords of wood in him and over in the corner under one of his rib bones was a Jew peddler with his merchandise spread on a table and the peddler looked out and said, "Sale today, good brogan shoes at $1.99."

And so we two liars would carry on our contest as long as we could make up lies or until the audience got tired of us, and the audience seldom did.

Fist and Skull

"There is nothing like a lightning fist and skull tangle to work the grudge out of a man," said Uncle Robert Light to me one day. "Yessir. I can remember 'way back to right after the Civil War when I was a gosling boy. I had a bad fight with Len Ragland. I was standing on the school ground at Crowder's Grove when Len slipped up behind me and tripped me up. Ah-ee, I was never hurt so bad in all my born days. He liked to have killed me. I swore then that some day I'd get it back on him—I'd whip him if it was the last thing I ever did. Well, his family moved out'n the Harnett country down below Fayetteville, and I didn't see him for some long eighteen years. Come to think of it, it might have been fifteen years, but it was a long time. Then one day I met up with him down at Uncle Josh's ferry on the river. I was coming out of Summerville and he was going toward town. We recognized each other. Yes, we did. I was riding a horse and had a pistol strapped around me. I was a deputy sheriff then. I stopped the horse and called out to Len. 'Well, Len,' I said, 'it's been long enough now and we might as well settle our little matter.' So I got down and started taking off my coat. 'Great God, Bob,' he said, 'what's it all about?' And I told him. 'Lord ha' mercy,' he said. 'You sure can hold a grudge a long time.' 'Yeh,' I said, 'and if you had been hurt that day as bad as I was, you'd hold a grudge a long time. You liked to've killed me when you strapped my skull against the ground, and I never forgot it.' 'But, Lord, Bob,' he said, 'you're an officer now and I can't fight an officer.' 'I ain't no officer no longer,' I said, and I pulled off my badge and flung it on the ground. 'But you got a pistol too,' he said. 'No, I ain't got a pistol,' I said. I unstrapped it and laid it aside. 'Come on, Len,' I said.

"And we went to it.

"Well, sir, I'm here to tell you that fellow near 'bout killed me again. He was a man! And I was a man too! I weighed a hundred and eighty-five in them days and had done a little boxing on the side. And I can tell you we tore up the ground down there by the river that day—Len and me did.

Ah-ee, he was a much man! And as I said, he near 'bout killed me again.

"We finally quit. I helped him up in his road cart, and I got on my horse somehow and made it home. And the only part of my shirt that was left was the collarband with a piece of my necktie rolled in it.

"Well, after that, next Sunday, or a few Sundays after—as soon as we were able to get about—we met at the church. And he was a sight to see! He was walking all trembly like with two walking sticks and his head was sorter crank-sided. It pleased me so to see him in that condition that I felt right friendly toward him. We shook hands and called it square. And we kept good friends until the day he died. You know what they put on his tombstone—some words that I told 'em to put—'The bravest man I ever knew and the truest friend I ever had.' "

MacNeill's Oath

When William Jennings Bryan was running for president, Phil MacNeill vowed an oath he would never cut his beard until Bryan was elected. Year after year went by as Bryan kept being defeated and Phil's beard grew longer and longer. Phil was a sensitive fellow and his long beard began to embarrass him, and he appeared less and less in public. Finally he moved far out in the sand-barrens in western Harnett and put up as a hermit in a little shack, eking some sort of a poor living there from his sandy hillside. I visited him in his old age. The side road leading to his shack had grown up in blackjack and sassafras bushes and I had to park my Ford and push on through the briars and thickets afoot as best I could. Phil met me in front of his shack—blear-eyed and incredibly dirty, beard and all. We sat down under an oak tree and he began reciting Burns's poetry. "John Barleycorn is dead," he sang up toward the branches of the sheltering oak. Later he showed me his sleeping place—a pallet on the floor of a little log smokehouse. His dwelling nearby—a somewhat better building—was locked up. He had for a pillow a single piece of oak log with an old ragged man's coat thrown over it. The pallet was placed in front of the fireplace, and the fireplace was open to the weather at the back, for the stick-and-dirt chimney had fallen down.

"I don't sleep in that there house," he said pointing to the dwelling off a few yards. "The ha'nts run about so that I can't sleep, so a year or two ago I moved out here in the cookhouse."

"What sort of ha'nts, Mr. MacNeill?"

"Oh, I don't know—just ha'nts. At night you could hear 'em running and running just like big rats. I couldn't stand it. So I come out here."

"You sleep pretty well here?" and I gestured.

"No, I don't sleep much a-tall. Old Anarchy bothers me so."

"Anarchy?"

"Yeh, between old Anarchy and the ha'nts I have been having a tough time. Let me show you." And he stood suddenly up and dropped his dirty trousers down and there was his hip all raw and festered—a terrible sight. I jumped up.

"Good gracious, Mr. Phil, you're hurt bad! How in the world did that happen?"

"Like I told you," he said looking down at the terrible

raw flesh coldly and peeringly, "Anarchy." And he went on. "About a week ago while I was lying trying to sleep—I usually keep a little bit of fire going in the fireplace to keep me warm—maybe dozing some—old Anarchy crept up outside the house, reached in and put a handful of fiery punk inside my britches. When I come to I was all afire and the side of my hip was burnt clean off."

"I'm going to get you to a doctor!" I declared.

"Nunh-uh, you ain't either," he answered stoutly, and he jerked his trousers up, buttoned their one front button, and hooked his old greasy belt tight again. Then staring off he broke into another recitation.—" 'My luve is like a red, red rose, so early sprung in June.' I got to go back to chopping my corn," he said abruptly and turned. He limped swiftly away, picking up an old broken-handled hoe lying on a log as he went. I stood looking after him. "My corn needs chopping bad," he called back, and on he went out into a scattering of little pine trees and there he began to chop, and I noticed some feeble little stalks of corn which he had planted here and there among the pines.

I turned away and mournful were my thoughts as I walked back to my Ford.

During the winter a heavy snow fell in the sand-barrens, and the county dirt roads were shut off for a week or two. I kept thinking about the hermit of Harnett and when the snow melted I went down to inquire. Phil MacNeill was already dead. A distant neighbor seeing buzzards roosting on top of his house, cold as it was, went to inquire and found him lying stiff and stark in his cookhouse with his great bearded head on his wooden log. Old Anarchy was finished with him.

Devil's Lane

Two brothers in the Valley, John and Young Honeycutt, didn't do any killing over their strip of devil's lane, but they did a lot of lawing, thus doing grievous financial damage as the years passed. Each of them laid claim to a little hog-run along their property line and were in constant suit about it. Again and again they would be listed in the county paper court docket as Honeycutt *vs.* Honeycutt. The trial would be held and one would win a victory. Then the other would file a countersuit. So it was that as time went on, the village lawyers got the major part of their cotton and tobacco money.

One August at an especially fervent protracted meeting held by that mighty preacher, hairy Neill Hodge, the two brothers got converted. So all filled with brotherly love and spiritual grace now, they met, hugged each other, and wept and boo-hooed in each other's arms.

That evening when they got back home these newly washed and purified souls went out to have a look at the strip of land, which by this time had become well known in the neighborhood as "the Devil's Lane." Standing there side by side and in good fellowship and with their tears dried, they considered the cause of their animosity, and their conversation ran as follows.

"I'll declare," said John or Young, it makes no difference which, "ain't it a sight to think that you and me all these years have been suing one another over this little old bitty piece of land?"

"That it is. It's a sight," said Young, "yeh, a shame and a scandal."

"I been thinking a lot since we stood up for the right hand of fellowship at church this morning," said John.

"So have I too," said Young.

"And I tell you what I'm going to do," said John. "I'm going to give up my part of this Devil's Lane complete. I want you to have it."

"That's what I been thinking about," says Young. "I want you to have it, John."

"Nah, nah," said John, "It's yours, Young. I give it to you and I'll have the deed drawed come Monday morning in the courthouse, denoting it's yours."

"No, I can't allow that," says Young. "I'll have the deed drawed in your name."

"Dad blame it," said John, getting a little testy. "It's yours, Young."

"Well, dadgum," said Young, "it's your'n, John, and that's the last I want to hear about it. Your'n!"

"I won't take it," says John.

"Yes, you will," says Young.

"You got to take it yourself," said John, "and that'll show you there ain't no more hard feeling in my heart agin' you and that I'm gonna live in a state of grace from now on."

"No, you take it, and that'll show you how I feel and am gonna live."

"I'm the oldest," said John, "and my word ought to count. It's your'n."

"You remember what Pa used to say, John. He said, 'John, Young may be younger than you in years, but he's got a better head on him.' "

"Well, I reckon I ain't never heard of that before," says John, getting a little more ficety-like.

"Well, that's what Pa said, and I say on account of my judgment being better—"

"Your judgment ain't better," says John. "I deny that on a stack of Bibles a mile high."

"So you don't think Pa said it, do you?" says Young, getting somewhat red in the face.

"No, I don't," says John. "I don't believe he said it."

"Well, I reckon you know what that makes me," says Young, "makes me out an outdacious liar."

"Well!" says John.

"Well!" says Young. And there they stood looking at each other, their eyes turning red as a terrapin's. And Young hitched up his britches and his hands quiled themselves up into two fists. "Ain't nobody ever called me a liar before and got away with it," he says.

"And I reckon there ain't nobody that ever drawed back his fists that made me take cover," said John. And with that they squared off and started walking around each other like two game roosters looking for the first chance to make an attack. Seeing an opening, Young suddenly hauled off and ker-blip let John have it by the burr of the ear. That brought him down to his knees and Young flew on him, but John came back butting at him and got him in the pit of the stomach and piled him over in the weeds.

And from then on they had it, fighting and gouging. Finally some neighbors come along and separated them or I reckon they would have killed each other. For by that time Young was chewing on John's ear and had it about half-eaten off and John had got one of Young's long fingers in his mouth and was chewing it to a pulp.

At the next term of court there was the same old notice in the newspaper, "Honeycutt *vs.* Honeycutt," and assault and battery was the charge this time, one against the other.

They were tried in the court and both put under a peace bond, and the judge had the lane resurveyed. A line was run down the middle of it, and the court ordered a fence put up along the line. Now for a good long time John and

Young have lived at peace, and each one still stays on his side of the wire fence.

But since the big fight between them, neither one has been the man he once was. The side of John's head is still disfigured, his ear looking like a dried-up prune, and Young's hand is about half useless because the long finger John chewed on remains stuck out, stiff as a stick and useless.

Old Dan Truelove, the ninety-year-old surveyor and godless liquor reprobate, said that's what they got for messing with religion. If they had stayed away from that preacher, he said, they'd be hale, hearty men to this day. But then old Dan didn't have much more character than an egg-thieving dog, being a tattletale and liar the way he was, and no attention was paid to him. And besides, as everybody knew, he was drinking himself fast into the grave and had been doing so for the last fifty years.

Dueling

"Yes," said Uncle Myron Lassiter as we were sitting by his fire one winter night, "fighting duels has long gone out of fashion—between individuals—men, that is. But the nations keep on doing it crazy as ever. It takes humanity in the mass a lot longer to learn anything than it does a man singly, I reckon.

"Well, old Miles Stevens was a big landowner here in the Valley before the Civil War and owned a lot of slaves to boot. He was one of the most highfalutin and prideful men, my daddy said, that ever was. After the war his slaves were freed, but it seemed to make no difference to old Miles. He was just as proud and overbearing as ever. Though his worldly goods had shrunk mightily, he still kept his aristocratic ways and lorded it over folks. He used to wear a wide white pleated shirt and top hat and a wing collar and tie that looked like a bolt of black ribbon tied around his neck, and he carried a silver-headed walking stick and wore a square coat that hung down like the one Governor Hoey now wears. Perhaps the most noted feature about him though was his nose, big and red and I mean red—maybe from drinking so much cherry bounce when he could get it. And wherever old Miles appeared—him and his big face and nose and clothes—he made an impression on everybody. As I say, he was an aristocrat of the old South, sure enough. And as for size he was well over six feet high and weighed nigh to three hundred pounds, my daddy said.

"He lived up there in Haywood, and Haywood was right much of a town in the old days. Must have been five or six hundred people there. It was built in the forks where the Haw and Deep Rivers come together to make the Cape Fear. There were three churches, a Presbyterian church, a Baptist church, and a Methodist. Might have been an Episcopalian too, but I disremember. But anyhow, I know there were at least three churches. And there was a drugstore and a big hotel run by old Captain Brown—but it's all passed away now and gone."

"I was out there a few years ago and saw the remnants of the old hotel," I said.

"Yes, there was a big hotel and mighty fine houses there, a race track and plenty of betting and gambling and cockfighting going on in those days. The aristocratic Scotchmen from down toward Fayetteville and Wilmington would come up there in the summer with their families to get away from the chills and fever down in the lowland. And so old Haywood was right much of a place and had a lot of big folks in it, as I say.

"About the biggest one in it of course was old Miles Stevens. Now there was another special fellow there in Haywood and no aristocrat. His name was Bob Jefferson. In fact, he was a grandson of one of the poor white Jeffersons who had been a bound boy in his young days to old Miles's father. Bob had the stuff in him, though, and he had worked himself up and finally got a pretty good grocery store. Miles would run up an account there in the store and wouldn't pay him. Bob would send him a notice and old Miles would ignore it. Sometimes he'd meet Miles on the street and tip his hat polite enough and say, 'Mr. Miles, I'm needing that account settled mighty bad.' And Miles would look down his big nose at him and nod, and say, 'I'll be taking care of it right away as soon as I get some money that is overdue me from my investments.' And in fact he did now and then pay a little on his debt, if he happened to sell a bit of timber off his dwindling piece of land. But all the time his indebtedness to Bob increased.

"Finally, young Bob lost his patience. He was a kind of waggish fellow, too, and one day when old Miles come walking into his store in his pompous way and started to pick up some oranges and English walnuts and put them in a paper bag without a by-your-leave, Bob's temper began to boil. Miles had his Negro boy with him to tote the groceries and fruit home, and poor Bob just didn't have the grit to tell him no, for all his boiling. But while he was standing there, with old Miles getting his groceries together, his mind was a-working. So when he weighed the groceries and handed them over to old Miles who leant over to take 'em, what did Bob do? He just reached out and grabbed old Miles by his big nose and give it a terrible twist to right and left and made it pop. Then he broke out laughing.

"Well, that was a foolish thing to do, as you might imagine. And why Bob done that I don't know. Maybe it was just some kind of a wild impulse that made him seize it all of a sudden. Anyhow, as I said, old Miles's nose had got to be much like a headlight from his drinking so much cherry bounce and highland liquor, and maybe it stood out like the challenge of a headlight or something. Anyhow, when Bob give it that twist, Miles let out a yell. He staggered back, dropped his groceries and with his hand to his tortured member declared to all and sundry that his honor had been insulted.

"Bob then said he didn't care a hoot about his honor, he wanted his money. His courage had begun to rise by this time, I reckon. Old Miles couldn't take that, so with his insulted honor he drew himself up to his full six feet and more and said, 'I challenge you to a duel, seh. My seconds will wait on you. I bid you good day!' And he swept out of the store swirling his cane in front of him. The Negro boy grabbed up the groceries and followed.

"One of the neighbors, acting as Miles's second, did come down and have a huddle with Bob. He might have been beholden to Bob, I don't know, he and Bob fairly cooked up a deal between them—after Bob had cussed old Miles out and said the damned scoundrel hadn't paid a red brownie on his bill in eighteen months, and he'd do anything to get even with him, for he knew he never was going to pay it. Of course, the duel business had been outlawed in North Carolina fifty years, even before that, but old Miles's honor went away back beyond the outlawing, and so he resorted to this manner of settlement.

"Now according to the law of dueling, I've been told (and old Miles knew all about it), the challenged man, that is, Bob, had the right of choosing the weapons. So Bob ups and tells the second that he would choose blunderbuss pistols. He had a couple of these old critters that had been given to him by an old soldier, and he had them back there in the store. So they brought 'em out and figured out how to load 'em with cap and ball and get ready for the duel.

"Well, down that way," and Uncle Myron gestured, "lived Dr. Wyche. He was an awful good doctor, that fellow was, and they called on him and put him onto the secret, and the secret was this—they would go through with the duel, but they would make the whole thing a prank. At Bob's suggestion, thinking of that big white shirt front, no doubt, they decided to load one of the big blunderbusses with a terrible charge of ripe pokeberries, for it was the time of the year for them and they were all standing around in the fence jambs just hanging down. That would be Bob's pistol. The other one would have only a charge of powder and paper wadding in it.

"So, next morning, bright and early, they met as planned out on the field of honor—a potato patch—some distance outside of Haywood. Dr. Wyche was there with his instrument case. He opened it up and laid his saws and forceps and bandages out while the seconds conferred. And old Miles, as grim and as grave as a judge, and with a special white shirt on now, shining brighter than ever, all ironed up with his collar and big black tie accompanying for the occasion—was waiting directions.

" 'These are your instructions, gentlemen,' the seconds said. 'You will stand back to back with your pistols raised, and you'll march eight paces, and at the word "fire," turn and fire.'

"Old Miles put a devastating eye on Bob and asked did he have any last words that he wanted to say on earth. 'That's just what I was going to ask you, sir,' said Bob. His teeth were chattering, and he was acting like a man scared out of his wits. He knew old Miles's pistol didn't have a thing in it but a charge of powder and paper while his own was loaded with an extra heavy charge of powder and the rest of the barrel jammed tight with a long wad of them ripe pokeberries. But he acted scared just the same.

"So they put themselves back to back and the seconds counted. The two opponents started walking away, and at the word 'fire' they turned and fired. And they said it sounded like two small cannon had gone off. Well sir, that charge of pokeberries come out of Bob's gun in such a terrific wad and at such speed, it hit old Miles right smack on that shirt bosom, spattered all over his face and knocked him flat on his back. His own blunderbuss had just fired paper into the air, of course.

"They all rushed up to Miles and made a terrible to-do over him, whooping and hollering and carrying on. Now old Miles's wife and daughter had got word of the duel and they had pleaded with him not to go through with it, but he had insisted, and the wife was at home that very minute, weeping and grieving. It happened that Miles's granddaughter, Lucy Belle Bryant, whose parents lived in Raleigh, was visiting the Stevenses at this time, and she had added her voice trying to persuade the old man from his foolish and dangerous course. But no go. And so unbeknownst to Miles, Lucy Belle and his old-maid daughter Pearl had followed to the field of honor at a distance and hid themselves behind a tree nearby. When Pearl saw her daddy fall and with a terrible mess of blood all over his shirt and splashed up in his face, she let out a scream and started back across the fields home, crying as loud as she could, 'Lord God, Mom, he's shot, Papa's shot clean through the heart, and his blood and brains are splattered all over him!' And she run wailing through the town telling the dreadful news. But Lucy Belle hurried over to the fallen grandfather. And that's how she and Bob Jefferson first met up with each other.

"So it was they laid old Miles out under a tree and were gathered sorrowful around him. And Lucy Belle tried to kneel by him and do what she could, but Bob with his arm around her lifted her away and said it was too terrible a sight for her to endure. He no doubt was afraid for her to get too close to Miles right then for she might get onto the fact that all the blood was nothing but a fake. And too she was mighty purty, and maybe Bob didn't mind lifting her away just to be doing it. The fellows took off their hats now, and the doctor knelt by and examined Miles. And Bob stood there holding Lucy Belle by the hand to keep her from getting too close, his face all broke up and saying he never meant no harm and was sorry as he could be. The doctor told Miles how he didn't 'spect he had long to be on earth, did he have any last words, any unfinished business to attend to.

"Well, the old scoundrel said maybe he hadn't lived just right but at the time he couldn't think of any particular sins he had committed lately and the old Moster would have to take him as he was, bless his name, for he would understand and pardon the weakness of the flesh and his love for his dram which he had been taking as a morning pyeartner for his health's sake—lo these many years—Amen. And then Bob, mad as hops, asked him what about that bill he owed at the store. Old Miles said yes, it was a sin, that was, that he hadn't paid it. He realized it now, he said, and he didn't want to go to meet his Maker with that on his conscience and that he had a little money from the last turpentine he had sold and to tell his wife, his brokenhearted widow and his desolated daughter and weeping granddaughter here, to take care of this debt, because after all it was a debt of honor.

"But the granddaughter Lucy Belle there wasn't really weeping now, for by Bob's winking at her and making some signs to her with his hands where Miles couldn't see, she was beginning to catch on, and so she was more pretending to weep than not.

"And then Bob called on all to witness that the dying man had promised that his debt at the store would be paid. And they all said 'That's right,' they were witness to the fact and they'd see to it that the debt was paid.

"After this then they all broke out laughing, and it didn't take old Miles but a minute to catch on. And he didn't say a word. He was fighting mad, but he didn't say a word. He climbed to his feet, got his hat and cane and marched straight off, walking proud as ever to his buggy and so drove away. Bob had to take Lucy Belle home in his buggy, and that's how their courtship began.

"Well, in no time the story was everywhere, and the people were bending up and down and shouting and hollering in fun all along the streets of Haywood. Old Miles took to his house and stayed shut up for weeks. But finally his proud spirit broke down, and he came forth again. And in church on Sunday he stood up in front of everybody and acknowledged his foolishness and sinfulness, saying that from this time forth he was going to live a different and better life. So he said, and people believed him—for awhile they did. But to tell you the truth, he didn't change one iota, and when he died a couple of years later he still owed his account to Bob. But Bob said he didn't mind now, not at all, in fact he considered the account paid in full and more than in full and had marked it off the books, for out of it all he got Lucy Belle for a loving wife."

The Corn Shucking

In the old days when late October and early November came on, the farmers would haul the corn in the shuck from the fields, pile it in a horseshoe-shaped mounding around the barn door, and invite their neighbors in to help shuck it. This was always a joyous and festive occasion, and the housewives would cook up a storm of ham, barbecue, beef stew, chicken, pastry, pies, cakes, biscuits, and a multitude of things for good eating and fun. The shuckers usually ate in sequent groups—the oldest men first and the younger and yearling fellows last. Sometimes after the supper feeding was over, the girls would come out to the cornpile and find their respective sweethearts and snuggle down beside them and pretend to help shuck corn. After that, of course, the falling of the shucked ears toward the barndoor slackened down considerably. Now and then someone would find a red ear, and then a forfeit—or better, a reward—of a kiss would be taken by the young people—to the merriment and good spirits of all.

One corn shucking occasion I especially remember. I was about seventeen at the time and much in love with a country girl. I could hardly think of anything else, except maybe poetry. One cold October evening as the sun was going down in its great splurge of fire across our wide fields, I was out in the lot milking the cow, and the girl's little brother came by riding his father's black mule.

"Gonna shuck corn tomorrow night and want you all to come," the ruffian said, letting loose a squirt of tobacco juice at the gate post and eyeing me sternly from beneath his mop of tangled blond hair.

Keeping back my eagerness, I answered with due deliberation and judicial gravity that some of us would try to be there. Of course I'd be there if torment—if hell didn't freeze over.

I watched my time, and the next afternoon when everybody was out of the house, I slipped in and got my daddy's razor and took my first shave as best I could. Then I slicked down my hair and put on my Sunday suit—all for the girl's sake—and stood ready to ride. As a last measure I sprayed myself plentifully with my sister's cologne too. Then I hitched up my mule and drove through the country, feeling fit and ready as a man of God.

The corn shucking was in full swing when I got there. Young men, old men and boys were sitting and squatting around the horseshoe pile. In the dusk the stripped ears were pouring over toward the barn like a thick swarm of dancing bats.

I took my place among the sweaty overalls and ragged hats. Out of my vest pocket I fished my string-fastened shucking-peg, made of the hardest dogwood, seasoned by sun and fires, and coming to a fine point at the end. In a few minutes I was ripping the shucks open and shooting the ears over with the best of them. On and on we shucked, ear by ear, nubbin after nubbin, throwing the shuck behind with one hand and reaching forward with the other. And all the while there was a low drumming and seedy spattering of the corn falling ever toward the crib.

I was thinking about the girl in the house as I shucked, seeing her in my mind as she helped arrange the table, dishing up the stew and all the fine things to eat. It was almost time for supper now. The fields out by the barn were growing dim, and the open door to the hayloft above was a square of blackness, and looked lonesome. I gazed up at the sky and saw that the stars were coming out. The sky looked lonesome too. That was a trait I had—when I thought of something sweet and happy, I always thought of something sad and lonesome. One feeling seemed to bring on the other.

"Let's sing some," I said timidly to Laughing Gus Brown. "Sam Adams and Tim Messer's here."

Sam and Tim and Gus and I had been singing as a country quartet now for some time—round at corn shuckings, ice cream suppers, parties, and the like. We sure could make music, if I do say so.

Presently Tim and Sam left their places and came around. We made room for them.

"What shall it be?" said Sam, dumping his chew of tobacco into his hand and throwing it behind him.

"Oh, anything," I answered. "What would you like?"

"Sing about poor 'Omi," old Yen Yarborough spoke up in his chair a few paces away. Old Yen liked music, and he specially liked that mournful piece. He'd seen a lot of trouble in his time and now was dying from a bad sore that had eaten away most of his nose. Try doctors, herbs, salves, all that he might, including Miss Zua Smith's powerful plasters—nothing did him any good. But he still kept cheerful and wore his big bandage with dignity.

"Poor 'Omi it shall be," said Sam.

Thereupon we cleared our throats and settled our knees more firmly in the bed of shucks.

"Ta-la-la-la," said Tim, setting the chord. He was the first tenor and a good one.

"Do, sol, mi, do," growled Sam,

Then we let loose a harmony that shattered the twilight air and trembled the cobwebs in the hayloft. Out, around, and upward we sent the lady's plaintive story.

> "O pity, O pity! pray spare your babe's life,
> And I will deny it and not be your wife."
> "No pity, no pity, no pity have I,
> In yonder Deep River your body shall lie."

How we did make it chord, all with queer minor and mode! And when we'd reached the end where the poor lady's body, by desperate deed foredone, is found in the "drean" below the mill dam and the guilty George Lewis is captured and bound down in chains, there were grunts of approval and clapping of hands on all sides.

Then through the cool October evening I heard a voice that thrilled me to the bone.

"Come on in to supper, you all!" She was outside the lot fence with some other girls.

"Come on to supper!" the call was repeated.

The fellows around the cornpile craned their necks around, snickered and stirred with enlivenment. The older men would eat first, and seven or eight of them soon rose, dusted the corn silks from their clothes, and went on toward the gate.

"We need four more," old Yen called back.

And finally four middle-aged fellows followed the older ones to supper. The young girls in their white dresses and ribbons clustered around like beautiful butterflies beyond the fence.

"There she is," and Laughing Gus punched me in the side.

But I went on with my shucking as cold and indifferent as the old dummy that lived by the creek.

"You gals come over here and help us shuck this corn!" three or four voices called.

The group of girls beyond the fence were suddenly animated with a flurry of motion, and there were giggles and whispers among them. Finally little Cissy Tatum, who had a tongue like a scorpion's tail, shrilled out—"Who's that all dressed up in his wedding garments?"

A great shout went up around the corn pile, and I felt my face grow hot as fire.

"Come here, little Black-Eyes, and hold her hand!" cried Gus, who seemed to have gone crazy in his head. "Bring your handkerchief and an'int it, for she smells like the Queen of Sheby."

Sam Adams suddenly rolled over on his back and wallowed among the shucks with little squeals and whimpers of joy.

If only the ground would open and swallow me up, or if I might but burrow my way deep under the corn and hide myself from all human eyes! I remembered foolishly that Enoch walked with God and was not, for God took him. And so it was with Elijah—translated. I looked up at the sky and wished, as the Negroes sang—wisht I had-a wings for to fly. Then the girls went away, and she called back over her shoulder. "We'll all come and help you after supper."

"Do," shouted Gus, "and a kiss for every red ear!"

Soon the men came back and it was the turn of us younger

ones to go to supper. Sam and Gus had just made a bet about who could eat the most, and there was much arguing as to the powers of each as we went out of the lot.

"Sam'll do it."

"No, Gus will. He's got more room 'twist his ribs and his waist and is ga'ntlike."

We shuffled on through the darkness and crowded around the pump outside the dining room. There we washed up with strong homemade soap and dried our hands and faces on towels hanging from the limbs of a pecan tree. The young girls hovered about in the gloom and waited upon us as if we had been lords.

"Here's some soap, Charlie," one said shyly to her husky sweetheart.

"And here's a towel," said another.

"Hurry up there," the sharp voice of Miz McLaughlin called from the kitchen.

Through the lighted window of the parlor I could see other girls gathered, one playing the organ and singing, and two or three sitting on the lounge looking through the family albums. Time would hang heavy on their hands until we boys were through at the corn pile. Like a herd of goats we trampled in through the dining room and seated ourselves at the table. All the while I had not seen her.

Mr. McLaughlin was noted for his closeness, but he hadn't failed to provide on this occasion. No farmer does. The table was loaded down with chicken stew, ham, collards, early pork, beef stew and steak, biscuits, muffins, cornbread, potato pie, and custards and cakes, and goodness knows what all. Two or three stolid Negro women moved about the room, handing the dishes on. And over it all Miz McLaughlin, with face as dried as a bean root, watched with hawklike eye. She was a stingy one, no doubt, but she did urge everybody to help himself. If she cared for her rations, as it was said, she was due to suffer this night. And so we began. I being so timid, and with my mind on something else, the girl, like a fool got a whole plateful of collards from the first Negro woman. I hated "greens" above all things, and in a few minutes my appetite was gone. It looked like a grimace of pleasure on the hostess's face when I soon had to say "no" to a proffered dish of stew.

After a few minutes the girl came in and shyly spoke to Sam.

"Are you going to play for us later?" she said.

"We are if we can tote our vittles," he answered.

A bit longer she stayed in the room and then went off along the porch toward the parlor. Not once had I looked up at her, but sat bent over my plate diddling with the hated greens.

"Come on there, Samuel, my son, how many cups of coffee does that make you?" queried Gus.

"Six."

"I'm two ahead of you. Undo your belt. Heigh, Mis' Sally," he called to Miz McLaughlin, "fire up the b'ilers and put on more coffee."

"You boys'll kill yourselves," she murmured.

"Huhp, not hardly," said Gus. "I ain't had a bite all day. Been laying up for these here vittles. Ain't that right, Sam?"

"Put on another pot of coffee, Ellen," she said resignedly. The Negro woman went out into the kitchen.

"Now for the 'tater custard," Gus chuckled.

By this time several of the boys had returned to the lot. But I waited around to see the fun and maybe to see her when she came in again. It was touch and go with Sam and Gus as to who would win. Sam was short and thick, Gus was long and stringy. While they devoured plate after plate of the good things, Tim Messer, who had long ago finished, sat with a stub of pencil and an old envelope keeping tally.

"You boys'll eat me out'n house and home," Miz McLaughlin laughed mournfully.

"Not hardly," Gus chortled. "Lord, your smokehouse is a-running over."

"How do they stand now?" she sighed presently. "And where is their raising?" she added spitefully.

Tim pored over his envelope.

"Purty nigh even," he answered, eyeing his scrawls with the air of the bookkeeper in the bank. "Sam has sunk away ten coffees, two plates of collards, three plates of stew, two pieces of ham, fourteen biscuits, a slab of steak, and nine whole custards."

"How's Gus?"

"Two biscuits ahead."

"Oh, my goodness gracious!"

A couple of custards later, Sam laid his knife down and sat looking at Gus with his mouth open.

"I got about enough," he murmured.

"Land a'mighty!" Gus cried in astonishment. "Where's your appetite? He's on the puny list, poor fellow."

"Bring on your custards," wheezed Sam. He took three in his hand, staggered out into the middle of the room and lay down on the floor. He lay there flat on his back, devouring them. Several of the girls came in and laughed at him, and Maisie Strickland, his shamed sweetheart, begged him to get up.

"I can't do no more for man nor country," he finally said. "Open the door there—I'm coming out." He crawled to his feet and stumbled from the room, his upper lip wrinkled back most sickeningly.

When Gus had emptied another pot of coffee and gone three biscuits and a custard farther, he pushed back his chair and stood up.

"Now that's what I call a sort of a supper," he said. He reared back his shoulders and strode from the room, never caring for Miz McLaughlin's sharp look that went after him. And the rest of us followed. We passed Sam leaning over the yard fence. "G'won, leave me alone," he spluttered.

Back at the corn pile we shucked and shucked. Presently the cold moon came up behind the barn and peered in our faces. Gus suggested another song, but I, who had grown mournful, said I didn't feel like it.

"And Sam's not here, anyhow," I said.

I was waiting and hoping she would come. Well, if she did she'd go and sit with somebody, not me, of course. The corn was dwindling away under our onslaught, we'd be through in a few minutes. Then I heard the tap of the latch in the gate, and the shout that went up around the pile told me the girls were there. Through the edge of my eye I saw them come in. My heart pounded in my ribs and nearly stifled me, but I kept at my task, erect and with the gravity of a stolid Indian. I saw them settle themselves here and there along the pile with their different sweethearts. Ah, it was all so foolish anyhow. I didn't care, I didn't. Why'n thunder had I dressed up like a fool? Then a cool sweet voice spoke up behind me.

"Let me sit with you," she said.

I gripped the ear I was shucking. "There's maybe some room here," I answered casually, making a place for her.

"Uh-uh," Gus snorted, "red ears, where are you hiding!" And he went on making funny remarks, but I heard nothing now. Here she was, right here beside me, and she chose me before the rest. My head was swimming, and all the fine speeches I had planned were lost in a hazy dreaminess. Bless the Lord if a sort of sleepiness didn't soon come over me. What ailed me anyhow? Then I felt her soft hand against mine among the shucks. And fire raced all over me. But—well—she was reaching for an ear maybe, sure, that was all. We shucked away in silence. She would say nothing either. Once Gus stuck a red ear at me.

"Now's your chance," he said. But I made no reply and Gus threw the ear scornfully toward the barn.

"How's everything at your house?" she finally said.

"Well as common."

I wanted to talk out and laugh and cut up like the others, but something weighed me down like lead. I was happy, but something weighed me down. Once or twice she looked at me intently and then presently shivered and stood up. "It's cold here," she said, "and I better get my fascinator." She went out through the gate, and Laughing Gus lay back and roared with glee.

"What's all the fun?" a neighbor queried.

"The cat's got the bridegroom's tongue," he cackled.

Now if I but had a sledge hammer or rail-splitting maul I'd kill that Laughing Gus Brown. I wouldn't mind caving his head in, not a bit in this world. A flood of wretchedness came over me. I was the biggest fool that ever wore shoes, no doubt about it. Well, out I would go.

And I did. I stumbled up and went toward the lot gate. I would go home and go to bed where I belonged. Catcalls and merry gibes followed me out and cut me to the quick. With a sob in my throat I went toward the fence where my mule was tied. I began re-hitching him to the buggy. As I was ready to drive off, she came out of the gloom with her shawl around her.

"Where are you going?" she asked.

"They're about through now and I'd better go on."

"Don't go, we're going to play and have some music in a little bit."

"I better leave," I muttered, but I stood making no move.

She came closer and laid her hand on my arm. Mechanically I tied the mule again and stood by her, silent. There were no words to be had now, fool!

"The moon's so beautiful," she murmured, "let's go walking down the lane. We'll come right back."

We went along, and soon she took my arm.

"The wheel ruts make hard walking—so," she said.

The moon looked down with smiling face as we walked, and the fields lay wide and peaceful on either side. There in the hedgerow the flowers stood dead and sere from the early frost. The yarrow that Achilles knew held up its blistered hands, and the proud old mullein nodded its gray fuzzy dry head at us from the shadowy fence jambs. I felt it all rather than saw any of it.

"It's a beautiful night," she murmured again. "Look at the man in the moon!"

"And everything all around us," I answered foolishly and in a choking voice. At the turn of the lane we stopped and leant against the fence. Presently she laid her hand on mine, and I caught it in a tight convulsive clutch.

"What's the matter?" she whispered. I looked down at her with shining eyes. "Oh, me!" she cried. And I put my arms gently around her then.

"That's all right, that's all right," I kept saying crazily. For a long while I held her so. Then more foolish words came stammering through my lips. "I've been thinking a whole lot. I'm gonna do something in this world, gonna be something somehow. I'll do it, do it for you, you wait and see. They can laugh at me—I don't care—I'll—"

"They don't laugh at you." She leaned her head timidly against my shoulder and I kissed her fabulous hair once.

"Let's go back," she said as if afraid. And I could feel her tremble. For a while we stood there, and then hand in hand we went up the lane toward the house. The music had already begun, the fiddle and banjo ringing out through the night. Boys and girls could be seen having fun on the porch. Near the barn I stopped and gestured around with a quick sweep of my arm.

"You know, I'm gonna do something."

"Yes, you will."

"I'm gonna write about all these things, make poems and such—tell 'em how purty—how beautiful it is—"

"Yes," she said, "yes, you will!"

And hand in hand again, we went on toward the house and toward our future together—as I foolishly believed.

Bernie and the Britches

Bernie Randall seemed the last person in the world to whom financial fortune might come. Nobody ever expected him to amount to much. He was awkward, timid, and uncertain, with his weak, friendly smile, and homely as an old shoe. His people were poor as whippoorwills and lived down by the railroad tracks just a block or so from where later Bernie had his livery stable and then still later his huge automobile agency and used-car lot. His father was sickly and a hopeless addict to the patent medicine bottle, and the responsibility of both parents fell pretty much on the thin shrinking shoulders of this their only child.

Bernie grew up a drudge. From the time he was six or seven he was running errands for his parents, sweeping leaves out of people's yards, hiring out to pick cotton in some of the fields that came up to the edge of the town, even trying to shine shoes, or standing on the corner, dumb and fearful on Saturday afternoons with an armful of "Grit" newspapers for sale. But through all his twistings and turnings of odd jobs, he never developed the sharpness and quickness that one usually associates with an American boy in such situations. Rather he continued his humble and lonely browbeaten way.

He got a little schooling somehow—enough to read and write and do fairly simple sums in arithmetic—and later when he was big enough for his daddy to swear him by the child labor law he got a job weaving in the cotton mill, and there he labored year after year. When he was about nineteen, May Eppinger came to work at one of the nearby looms. She was a pretty dimple-faced girl with a light laugh and a love for candy and milkshakes at the corner drugstore. Bernie fell deeply in love with her, and his devotion was doglike persistence. May had a lot of other boys swarming around her, and with whatever levity or even bursts of scorn she treated Bernie he continued his dreamings and devotions to her.

In time his parents died and left him alone in the little house that had been their home. It was a rented place and now Bernie indulged in some planning of his own. From his earnings he was able to make a mortgage deal with young Ed Weatherford down at the bank to buy the little place. So he started paying monthly installments on it. Every now and then he would extract a dollar or two from his thin savings and get a box of candy for May, and once or twice he was able to get ahead enough to take her to the state fair at Raleigh. But of course come wet weather or dry weather, rain or shine, he must somehow scrape up enough each month for his house payments. And regularly he would take his few dollars down to the bank and there hand them over to Miss Raeford the bookkeeper or to young Weatherford, who in a swift round business hand would write out the receipt and pass it through the grill to Bernie with a cool and pleasant air.

This young Weatherford was everything that Bernie was not. He was tall, handsome, educated at the university, and sure of a big future with the power and money he had inherited from his father.

Though May had numerous suitors, somehow time passed and she remained unmarried. Maybe the men liked courting her better than marrying her. Whether for weariness from working at the mill or whatnot, she finally gave in and married Bernie, and then began to take her ease in the little house down by the railroad track.

And Bernie liked for her to do that. "You've already done your share of hard work, Baby," he would say. He loved to call her Baby. And he treated her like a baby, and she purred with satisfaction and lay back cool and sweet.

One year, two years, went by and May was taking it easy and Bernie was working like a dog in the mills. But however hard he worked, his promotion was slow. He never could learn how to deal with people, become swift and to the point, authoritative, a manager. Others younger and less experienced passed him by and became floor bosses or loom inspectors or even superintendents. But poor Bernie mostly remained at his loom. He didn't worry too much though for after all he had May, and in his humble opinion it was quite fitting that others should become successful and he continue in the rut where he was, though he would never think of it as a rut.

But May began to complain about the little house. "It's not fit to live in," she said. "We've got to fix it up, it leaks like a sieve." And so the patient Bernie went down to the bank again and after long talking to young Weatherford, arranged to borrow $3,000 on the house and lot for their remodeling and improvement. So after succumbing to a stiff financing fee plus the regular 6 percent interest, he was ready to sign the papers, and following young Weatherford's instructions brought his wife May to sign with him. She was all dolled up for the occasion and it made Bernie proud to see that young Weatherford looked at her with admiring eyes.

The pinch on Bernie was harder now. It was tough making the monthly payments on the loan. And once when he fell sick and lost a few weeks from work, the first cold grip of despair got its bite into his stolid and lightless soul. He looked at Baby propped up in bed reading a murder serial in the newspapers and for once wrung his hands. "What am I going to do, Baby?" he queried.

"Oh, you'll make it somehow," came her light answer. "You

always do. And, say, I seen an ad in the paper yesterday for salesmen at forty dollars a week. That's ten dollars a week more'n you're making now," she said.

Bernie shook his head. The idea of being a salesman frightened him. But she insisted. "I bet Ed Weatherford—Mr. Ed would recommend you and help you get the job," she said.

"Not him," said Bernie. "All he studies is money—and women."

"Women?" she laughed.

Under her insistence Bernie went down and sure enough Ed Weatherford recommended him highly to the vacuum cleaner company and he got the job. And not only that, the bank lent him enough money on a second mortgage to get a second-hand Ford. And so Bernie's days as a vacuum cleaner salesman began. He worked hard at it. Nobody could deny that. He was up early and gone to distant points, here and yonder from farm to farm and village to village and from county to county, pushing his product.

The depression days were coming on down now and sales resistance was growing. He intensified his efforts. He was up earlier. He worked later and drove farther. But every night somehow he would get back home to his Baby. Sometimes when he was up and away at early dawn and an installment on the house was coming due at the bank, he would have to have May take the money and go down to Ed Weatherford and pay it.

Things tightened up all along the line now and the banks were pulling in their horns some. Young Weatherford himself would go out visiting among the farmers, foreclosing and collecting here and there. And sometimes he would come humming home at night in his blue Cadillac with quite a roll of money in his pocket, even as much as $5,000 it was said, to be deposited in his bank the next day.

That's the way it was with him. Whatever he went after he succeeded. And all the while poor Bernie Randall was coming down to his pitiful bankruptcy. One day he got up early to start one of his dreary rounds. He had heard that over in Wilson, a town some fifty or sixty miles away, there were several prospects. He told May he wouldn't be back that night and for her to get one of her sisters to come and stay with her. She laughed and said she wasn't afraid to stay by herself and she put out her pretty lips as usual in a rosebud pout as he kissed her goodbye.

"I'll be back tomorrow night," he said. And he rode off.

All day he drove through the virgin territory. But sales resistance was 100 percent. The tobacco market had just opened and the price was bad and the papers had given the prospects as being even less encouraging for the future. Late in the afternoon, completely whipped down, he decided to drive around by Raleigh and talk things over with the head office there. When he arrived, the first news that hit him between the eyes was that his agency was being canceled. A letter already was in the mail to him saying so. He turned in his sample cleaner and stumbled back to his little Ford car and sat there numbed and anguished. The darkness came down, the street lights flared on and still he sat staring at a black wall before him. And all the while he was thinking of how he had failed, miserably failed his sweet and precious Baby. Wait till he got home and told her the terrible news of what had happened to him. How could he break her heart like that. And in his mind he could see her lying in bed, beautiful and sweet, a wonder and joy for any man to be proud of.

"Yes, lying in bed," he said to himself. He wasn't trying to put meaning in the words. He was only reciting them to himself, and then suddenly they had a meaning and he didn't like the feeling that came over him, a new feeling.

For the first time in his life Bernie Randall began to feel sorry for himself. Maybe for the first time he was seeing himself as he really was, a poor plodding dull fellow, hard put on by others.

Later a policeman tapped on his car window and told him he would have to move. And so back through the night toward home Bernie drove.

"The bank will foreclose on me now," he moaned. "I know that Ed Weatherford. He will squash me like a mouse in a steel trap." Anger began to rage in him. "It's a bargain he'll get too when he gets my house. That's the way them fellows make their money. They get poor guys like me in their grip and gripe and then squeeze 'em and take away what they got. And then they turn around and sell it to somebody else for double what it's worth."

There must be some way out, there must be. He couldn't drag Baby down into complete poverty and have to start living all over again in a rented two-room mill shack and he back in the mill beaming away—from morning to evening beaming away, and the lint sucking into his lungs. But what, what could he do?

When he got within a block of his home he cut his rattletrap motor off and let the car roll silently up to the house as was his custom when coming home late. He was always careful not to wake Baby. He got out softly and walked along the grass up to the little front porch. He unlocked the door gently and went into the hall. Setting his little old pasteboard suitcase down quietly, he made his way along the little passageway to the bedroom. He felt for the door and opened it noiselessly and there in the dark he took off his coat and trousers and laid them on a chair as ever. And it was just like him, the awkward fellow he was, to bump into the chair and make a racket. And Baby's voice cried out in sheer and sudden terror from the big bed, "What's that!"

"Sh-sh, nobody but me, Baby," he said. There came a stifling, shaking noise from the bed. "I didn't mean to scare you," he said. "Wait'll I turn on the light."

"No! No!" And her voice was quick and frantic.

"What's the matter, Baby?" he said, all sympathy and concern.

"I've got the most awfulest headache," she said. "It's killing me, it is. I don't know what to do with it. Please, please don't turn on the light. My eyes would hurt so, my eyes!"

And he could hear her sitting up in bed and rocking from side to side.

And then in his concern he said he would get a hot pad or come and rub her head, and she pleaded with him not to do it but to go at once right down to the drugstore and get her some aspirin. "No, no," she said. "You'd better get me some Luminal, for his headache come on all of a sudden and it's killing me, busting my skull wide open with the pain of it nearbout! Oh! Oh!"

He told her that the drugstore would be closed that time of night but she said if he would hurry he could wake up Ned Sauls the druggist and get something to ease her, seeing that this was such an emergency. Poor Bernie was so upset that he began feeling around him hunting for his trousers on the chair. Finally he found them, pulled them on, grabbed up his coat and set off running down toward the drugstore some two blocks away. He threw gravel up on the second-story window and woke up Ned Sauls who came down grumbling and growling. The nervous and excited Bernie told him about Baby's sudden and violent sick headache and she had to have help right away.

"That's the first time I ever knowed she had headaches," said Ned Sauls as he grudged out some Luminal tablets. "That'll be fifty cents."

"You better charge it, Ned," said Bernie, humbly.

"I'd like to have cash if I could, Bernie, seeing how it is," he said.

Bernie had some change in his pocket but hated to spare even a fifty-cent piece at this time from his dwindling funds. But what had to be had to be. He reached into his pocket and then froze for an instant in his tracks. Slowly his hand came out of his pocket like a thing alive and of itself and in this hand he held before him Bernie saw a great roll of bills with a rubber band around them. He stared at the bills, a wad so big that his fingers and thumb would hardly shut around it. Ned looked at him with popping eyes.

"Jerusalem!" he finally exploded. "Business must have been good lately, Bernie!"

"Looks—er—like it," Bernie finally spoke up stutteringly.

"It does that! How much you got there? Oh, hush my big mouth!"

"Hah, hah, hah," said Bernie again, and he heard the sound of his own voice high and shrill.

Ned the druggist was looking at him with growing admiration in his face now. "Daggone my hide," he said. "You must be some salesman. I reckon that'll make folks eat their words. Sure, buddy, I'll charge it, charge it. Anytime you want anything, come and get it and I'll put it right on the books, yessir."

Bernie let his gaze travel downward. A shock went through his spare frame again though he made no outward sign.

He was wearing another man's trousers.

He finally turned away, pushing the roll of bulging bills back into his pocket. "Much obliged to you, Ned," he called and went on softly out of the store.

He took his time in walking home. It was only a short distance but a lot of things were happening in his head as he walked. Thoughts were flashing by one another, ideas happening, and gears inside were turning as they never had turned before.

When he got near the house, he tried to whistle. But his lips were so dry that he had to wet them with his tongue. And after several efforts he finally got out a stave or two of the only song he knew called "Beulah Land," which he had learned in Sunday School years before. Baby would hear him and know he was coming back. Then he saw that he didn't have to whistle anymore, for far down the sidewalk he discerned the figure of a man rapidly disappearing into the darkness. And he knew who the man was and he knew too that he was wearing away a pair of slick-seated dark britches with about two dollars change in the pockets.

Bernie doddled around outside the house for a while and then went into the kitchen and got a glass of cold water and took it to Baby. She was sitting up in bed in her blue lace nightgown with the light on, bent over and her arms wrapped around her knees. She didn't look up when he came into the room but just sat there.

"Here you are, Baby," he said, holding out the glass. "I got you the Luminal." She said nothing. "You got the light on now," he said. "Don't it hurt your eyes?"

"No, I'm feeling a little better now," she said. And she took the glass of water and swallowed a couple of Luminal tablets, then lay back in bed and pulled the covers up to her chin. "Have a good trip?" she finally inquired.

"Well, not so good at first," he said. "But maybe not so bad after all. I'll tell you about it tomorrow."

"All right," she said, "do. And come on to bed now."

He switched off the light and went out into the hall. He heard her body jackknife up in bed again as she called out, "Ain't you coming to bed here?"

"I'm going to lie down out here," he said. "I got some figuring to do." She said no more and he stretched himself out on the sofa which was set against the wall in the little combination entrance hall and living room. He lay there in the darkness, thinking, thinking. And presently he heard Baby begin her snuggy little snoring.

"Lordy mercy, she's already asleep!" he said to himself incredulously.

Presently he got up and with his shoes in his hand slipped out through the back door and sat on the steps looking out toward his small plot of vegetable garden. All night he sat there, and when the dawn was breaking and the chilly sparrows were chattering in the maples along the street, he went in and changed into his one remaining suit of clothes and came out with a package which he deposited in the incinerator in the yard and started a fire burning it. Then he returned to the house and began cooking breakfast.

Later in the morning he went down to the bank.

"Morning, Miss Raeford," he said, as he stood before the teller's window.

"Morning, Bernie," she said without too much respect in her voice. It was the same old thing. He had come about his small payments.

"I'd like to see Mr. Weatherford," he said.

"He's busy," she replied. "You can take the payments up with me as usual."

"I want to see him," said Bernie. His manner caused her to glance up, and he was looking at her straight and unblinking.

She went away and in a moment the door to an inner office opened and Weatherford appeared in it. He held the knob in his hand as if ready to step back and close the door at any moment. Bernie didn't smile. His face never changed, but there was a sort of queer smile deep in his soul to see Weatherford holding on to the knob.

"I thought," said Bernie, "I'd like to see you a little bit about my—about my mortgages."

"All right. What is it, Bernie?"

"I'd like to pay them off."

Weatherford was silent a moment, then spoke up strongly. "There's no hurry, Bernie. The bank is satisfied the way things are going, your paying by the month."

But Bernie said he was not satisfied and wanted to settle up "right here and now." Weatherford turned to Miss Raeford abruptly and told her to bring out the papers. The papers were brought and marked paid as Bernie counted out the full amount in greenbacks. Weatherford kept looking at him unblinking too and saying nothing.

"Thank you, Ed," Bernie said, as he put the canceled papers in his breast pocket. This was the first time he'd ever addressed the banker without a handle to his name.

"You're welcome," said Weatherford coldly.

"And I reckon this sort of squares things betwixt us," Bernie concluded.

"Well then—all right—glad it does," Weatherford said harshly.

And Bernie walked out of the bank a different man.

The depression came down more fiercely after this and began to wipe out Ed Weatherford's holdings. Like the fellows on Wall Street he had overextended himself. At the bottom of the market Bernie—with the $1,500 he still had left from the amount found in the britches—made a down payment on a farm at the edge of the town which had formerly belonged to Weatherford and the bank. He had confidence in himself now, and he held grimly onto it like a fice dog. And when the depression later lifted and money was easy again, he cut it up into building lots, sold them off, and made a killing. After this there was no stopping him.

Now in these later days as you come driving along the highway toward our town you are likely to see a good splashing sign carrying the big-lettered name of Bernard Randall, Dealer in Real Estate, Horses, Mules, Farm Equipment, and Fertilizer. And then when you get inside the town you are further confronted with Bernard Randall's success as a businessman. On the corner of Main and High Streets is Randall's hardware store, above which is the owner's suite of plush-furnished real estate offices. And farther south at the edge of the town by the railroad tracks is his huge auto business.

And as for Baby, well, she is completely changed now, and as everybody knows idolizes Bernie and can't do enough for him. She brings his slippers at night, she fixes his oatmeal in the morning, she mothers and waits on him as if he were a child. And he takes it all with never a word and never a sign to tell how he feels about her or anything else.

But in spite of all his business success, his fine new home, better clothes and such, he remains outwardly pretty much the same fellow he always was. He still speaks in his halting, awkward way and goes with slightly bent shoulders, his face still pale and freckled and his blue eyes dull as ever they were.

But he doesn't smile anymore, the way he used to do in his more humble days.

Archie and Angus and Their Churchly Work

Archie and Angus McNeill were identical twins and as alike as two persimmon seeds in the same persimmon or two peas in a pod. Not only did they look exactly alike and dress alike, but they behaved alike. They had the same motions and gestures and talked alike, voice for voice, and often used the same expressions. You want to remember that about the voice and expressions.

They were little men and supple and quick, and in their young days had the reputation of being fierce as bantam roosters and cocks of the walk in their manhood among the shady women in the upper section of the Valley where they lived. One summer Reverend Sandy King held a three-week revival in Little Bethel Church, and under the power of his preaching Archie and Angus both got converted good and hard from their sins. They took the right hand of fellowship, were baptized good and deep in MacDonald's millpond, and so set their faces clear and shining to serve their Lord.

For a long time the people had been wanting and needing an organ there in Little Bethel Church. And Reverend Mc-

Gregor, the regular pastor, felt that now since the congregation had been so much increased by Brother King's conversions, the time had come to get a good one and some new songbooks, too. Accordingly, the good members, old and new and especially the new, were called upon and exhorted to make pledges for the amount needed to buy the organ and the books. Under the spell of their new-found grace, and maybe because they had been such notorious sinners and wanted people to know they were 100 percent on the Lord's side now, Archie and Angus stuck up their hands and promised the final fifty dollars toward the purchase. It was a rather rash promise considering how hard money was to come by in those days, as time well proved. But, the Lord willing, they said to themselves, they would make the pledge good in the fall when the crops were housed.

The fall came along and the crops everywhere in that section of the Valley that year were picayunish and small. First there had been too much wet weather and then too much dry. And that was a queer thing too—to think that the one year Archie and Angus had tried to serve their Lord, He or whatever stood for Him had sent them the worst crop they'd ever had. They took notice of that fact betwixt themselves but tried to make the best of the situation instead of complaining against this Higher Authority. At the first killing frost they hauled their little bitty mess of peas, potatoes, and pork down to Fayetteville and sold them. But by the time they had paid the market and inspection charges and had their mule shod, they only had a dozen or so shillings left, as they called dimes in those days.

While they were sitting around in a cafe glum as sick herons and hungry enough in their bereft condition to eat the Lamb of God, as Bull Broadhuss used to put it, they heard a couple of half-drunk fellows laughing and talking a scandalous thing over in a corner. They were telling about a fast woman by the name of Mrs. Markham who ran a sort of fast house there in Fayetteville and had a standing bet that no man could outdo her in the bouts of love. Yes, she had a standing bet of fifty dollars for any man who would make her call for the calf rope of surrender. The twins sat there taking it all in, and they heard the fellows say that no man had ever been able to collect that bet and no man ever would.

"You hear that, Archie?" said Angus, or maybe Archie said it to Angus. It didn't make any difference which, since they were so identical in their feelings and thinking.

"Ah, the wickedness of creation!" said Archie.

"Worse'n Sodom and Gomorrah!" said Angus.

And then they looked at each other. The same idea was coming to them both.

"Like there's a sign in it," said Archie after a while.

"The Lord works in mysterious ways," said Angus.

"His wonders to perform," breathed Archie.

So of the same mind now, they wandered on up the street toward Mrs. Markham's place. It was night by this time and they finally stopped in front of the house, and there in the dark by the sidewalk hedges caucused a while, the way folks were wont to do at the Democratic Convention in Linneyville each campaign year. And so they made their plans.

"Certain to my soul 'twould be no sin!" said Angus.

"Seeing it's all for the cause anyhow," said Archie.

"And a service to righteousness," said Angus.

"And the wind and the weather bloweth where it listeth, as the Good Book says."

"And the Lord's rain falls on the just and unjust. And sometimes it don't fall at all!"

"Bless His name anyhow," said Archie humbly. "And the scriptures declare—be ye zealous in goodly works. Amen."

"Aye, lad, true, true—it do say in Hebrews ten that we should provoke unto love and do goodly works," said Angus.

So Angus took his courage in his hand, as you might say, and went into the house. Or it might have been Archie for all I know. It didn't make any difference which. And sure enough he found the lady waiting in her parlor. Angus said he was in bad need of a bed and restful comfort. And so with his projicking and hinting around with the widow and saying he had money coming in in the morning to match hers, the agreement was at last made and they started upstairs. She said she was willing to trust him but if his money wasn't there when she called for it she would have him where the hair was short and she meant short. Angus laughed and said wait till the play was played, having reference thereby to the old ballad of Sir Patrick Spence which in his sinful days he had loved so long. But her determined and certain manner kind of shook him in his shoes and set back his confidence. So he put up a little silent prayer for help and guidance as she led him along the hall and into her room.

Well, some time later he told the lady to please excuse him a minute, he had to get up and go out to the garden house to—er—answer the call of nature. Outside Archie was waiting.

"Well?" asked Archie.

"It's an undertaking, and we're up against it," answered Angus solemnly. "It's do or die for us. It's your time now."

"Aye," said Archie, forlornlike. And he suddenly shook hands with Angus as if he were departing for foreign parts, which he was.

"And ye'd better keep a kind of a little prayer going the while, Archie," said Angus. "I did—for a while."

"No, no, do pray tell!" said Archie hurriedly and alarmed.

"We've tackled several in our time, lad, but she's the wheel-hoss!"

"I will then if I can, but I misdoubt I'll be able to keep my mind on religious matters," said Archie.

"This is a religious matter!" said Angus sternly. "And while you're in there I think I'll eat me a snack of barbecue and oysters, short of money though we be."

"Aye, you do that, lad," said Archie kindly, "it might help." So he went in.

"You go and come mighty quick," said Mrs. Markham.

"Yea, I'm a brief man, and I move quick," said Archie. "And be not weary in well-doing, as the Scriptures put it."

"Lord have mercy, you ain't a preacher, are you?" asked the lady all shocked and aghast.

"No, ma'am, no," said Archie. "But someday I hope to be a deacon in Little Bethel Church."

So he put in his licks and some extra for the cause. And then he said excuse him, he had to go out to the garden house a minute to answer the call of nature but would be right back.

He met Angus along the hedge coming from his meal at the cafe. "Well?" Angus said, giving him a good look.

"Oom," said Archie, "make no mistake about it, we've got our hands full."

"Our calling and election's got to come from above," said Angus, "though we do all we can below! And you go down there and eat ye a quick snack too."

"Aye," said Archie. So Angus went in again.

And it kept up like that pretty much till daybreak, this visiting the widow and going out to answer the call of nature and eating in between. And finally the woman, stout as she was, hollered "calf rope!—eenough!" And when she paid over the fifty dollars, she turned up the lamp good and strong, saying, "I want to see what manner of man you be —that's played such havoc here tonight and no doubt ruined my garden house."

"I'm little but loud," said Angus—or Archie, whichever one it was—as he stowed the money away in his pocket.

"Loud!" moaned the woman. "You're the loudest thing that's ever put head in this place. And if you was full grown you'd be a plumb bucket of adders. Get gone from my house, and stay gone!"

"Why, bless my soul, you ain't on the puny list, are ye, Miz Markham?" said Angus—or Archie—all gleeful-like. He felt like bragging a bit now that he had the money all safe and won.

"And close the door soft when you leave," she croaked as she turned out the light, "for I want to sleep a week."

The next Sunday the Reverend McGregor stood up in Little Bethel Church and called for the pledges to be paid. And down the aisle marched Archie and Angus, proud as the two bantam roosters they were, their hair all slicked back and their faces and their collars shining with godliness. They laid the promised fifty dollars on the plate, and Reverend McGregor broke into jubilation. He called on the congregation to witness the deed of Brother Archie and Brother Angus.

"My friends," he said, "behold the goodly works of the Lord's true servants!"

"Amen," said Archie and Angus as they stood before the mercy seat, their eyes cast humbly down.

"Heavenly grace has blessed them mightily," said the preacher, "and their religion is where their pocketbook is."

Which is to say, the Reverend McGregor might be a good preacher, but as a carpenter with a measuring rule he would have been a much failure. He was off several inches.

You might wonder too what the church did when the story got out—as all stories finally do somehow, bless God! Well, it didn't do anything. For by that time Archie and Angus had been made deacons, and the organ was sounding mighty sweet when beautiful Belle Bethune played it Sundays, and the young and the old sang happily from their fine songbooks. So the people didn't make much of a to-do about it, except to tell the story on the sly—the way I'm telling it here—but with more of the details of goodly works in it no doubt.

And I hope it will keep on being told long after I am dead and gone, for it certainly was a thing.

Galloping Pneumonia

On one of my youthful forays in search of Valley folklore and stories, I called by to see my old friend, Mr. Mac, the miller on Upper Little River. Several neighbors were gathered around the big walnut tree that shaded the front of the mill, the while they waited for their corn to be ground, and they were talking of a sad occurrence over in town the day before. As was my custom I made some note of what they said.

Young Neill Arch MacNeill, one of the most popular young men in the neighborhood, had died rather suddenly of pneumonia in his father's house, they were saying. The funeral was to be held that afternoon in Old Tirzah Churchyard. They spoke of the pity of it all—this young man with a university education and the promise of a bright future in the law practice with his father, Colonel MacNeill, to be so suddenly cut off in the bloom of his early days. The discussion not only showed sympathy for the family's tragedy but a speculation also as to the exact nature of this cutting off.

"I misdoubt it were pneumonia at all," said Lammy O'Quinn from where he leant against his wagon body, whetting his lean hungry knife on the steel wagon wheel rim.

"It might be and it might not be," old Daryl MacCormack commented quietly from where he sat on a horse block turning a corncob quietly in his hand as if it might give him some reassuring opinion upon the subject.

"Sudden, I'll say so," said Russ Jones from his squatting position at the root of the tree. "Why only day before yestiddy I saw young Neill Arch coming out of Mangum's drugstore over there in town as spry as a gander, and he had a box of candy or something under his arm. A great big box."

Here Sassle Myers, the local cow doctor and pig-trimmer, let out a chuckle and gazed about him with a meaningful wink. He was standing on the opposite side of Lammy O'Quinn and whetting a still larger knife on the steel rim as if in preparation for a vast surgical onslaught upon all and sundry. "I bet you if you go over to a certain house there in town you'll find some of that candy right now if it's not et up by a sweet pretty mouth."

"They do say that woman loves candy," Lammy O'Quinn spoke up.

"An' that ain't all she loves," said Russ Jones.

"Ain't it the truth!" declared Sassle. And putting away his knife he pulled out a long flat adder-headed needle and began threading it with a piece of twine.

"It's all-fired sad and shocking, it is," said Lammy.

"He's dead and that's the size of it," murmured old Daryl. "Talking one way or another won't help it."

Here Mr. Mac came out of the mill and told them their meal was finished and he was done with grinding for the day.

"What's your opinion about young Neill Arch, Mr. Mac?" Sassle inquired, now looping the twine in an oval collar around the needle stuck in his jacket, as if to be ready for any sewing emergency or need.

"Yeah, don't it all seem kind of fishy to you?" Russ inquired.

They waited for the old miller to reply.

"Well," Mr. Mac said gravely, "a long time ago my grandmammy used to say there's only one way of coming into the world but a million ways of going out. Neill Arch took his own way out."

"And what is to be will be," said old Daryl, as he rose creakily from the horse block. "The scriptures spoke it long before any of us made our biddy peep into this world."

"But it's mighty hard on the Colonel," said Lammy.

"Yes, and it would be harder if by people's talking a scandal was started," said Mr. Mac pointedly.

"Right, right," said Sassle, "and we all agree with the report, don't we, folkses, that pneumonia was what carried him off, and galloping pneumonia at that?"

One or two voices said they agreed and one or two heads nodded the same.

When the neighbors had gone off in different directions home with their meal, I helped Mr. Mac sack up his tollings, and then we sat to the table and ate one of his fine lunches of garden vegetables and melons, interspaced with some of the beef stew he knew so well how to make. After that we went out and sat in the breeze under the walnut tree. He bit off a piece of his usual sweet flag and settled himself in his old rocking chair, chewing away with little goatlike workings of his chin.

"Looks like rain," he said, "them thunderheads there in the west."

"Yes, it does."

"Ever notice how often it happens to rain when a picnic or a funeral's on?" he queried.

"No sir, I had never thought of it," I said. "But I'll make a note of it."

"Yes, you do that," he chuckled. "There's no truth in it of course, but there's an old saying that it does so rain. Are you going to Neill Arch's funeral?"

"No, I'm not," I said. "There'll be a big crowd standing and gapping around, and crowds bother me. How about you?"

"No, I won't go either. We'll just sit here and talk."

For a good while he said nothing, sitting there chewing on his sweet flag and gazing out across the heat-filled fields. I waited patiently, hoping he would get back to the subject of young Neill Arch or maybe dig up from his remembrance a story of old times. Presently he spoke out.

"You know," he said, and he pulled his gaze from some far-off indefinite point in the field to let it rest on the toe of one of his brogan shoes, "the Indians here in the Valley had the right idea."

"I imagine they did, Mr. Mac," I replied vacuously.

"No doubt of it. They went to nature for their cures. Yes, sir, I've often thought that one of the worst things wrong with the modern world is all this new-fangled drug-store stuff they sell to body-conscious people. You might lay it down as a sort of law that nature-made medicine ninety-nine times out of a hundred is better than man-made."

Having said this, he lapsed into silence again and meditatively munched his sweet flag. I waited as before, wondering a bit what the subject of the Indians and their cures had to do with the death of young Neill Arch or any other subject to hand. After a moment he reached out and touched the bark of the walnut tree standing beside him as if it had been some sort of animal.

"Take this very walnut tree," he said, "nothing better than walnut juice for curing all sorts of skin diseases. That is, if you can stand the sting of it. My mammy used to doctor me when I had ringworm or tetter, and I'm here to tell you it would make me shout and call on the Lord. But it cured me, every time it did. Now take that red oak tree right out there in the edge of the woods. There's nothing better for man or beast at times than the inner red oak bark boiled into a brew. It's good for chickens too. I keep strips of the bark in the watering trough for my chickens all the time. It makes 'em lay better, keeps 'em toned up. And black draught is good too. That's a vegetable compound taken from mother earth's fields and hedges. I use it every now and then when I get to feeling sluggish. Have you ever tried it?"

"No, I never have."

"Well, you ought to. You can get it in town at the drug-store. That's one good thing they sell. My mother used to give it to us children. It's awful stuff to the taste but it sure does the work. And another thing we children used to take was sassafras tea. The Indians liked that too—and pennyroyal tea. In one of my old account books I've got a whole list of herbs and folk remedies set down. Maybe several hundred. Some of them I got from an old herb woman down near Fayetteville who's been doing all kinds of cures. They say she can cure cancers and tumors with a kind of plaster made of the herbs she gets in the fields and woods."

"I'd like to go down and see her sometime," I said.

"You can do that. Her name's Zua Smith. I told you about her once. You'll be able to get a mess of stuff for your plays and stories from her. Well, yes, black draught is good. And yesterday morning I went over to the drugstore in town to get me some, for I'd been feeling a little under the weather. And now I'll tell you what was told me, and since you're all the time studying human nature and writing about it, this maybe will come in handy for your use someday. But if you do use it you ought to change the names. Well, as I said, I went into the drugstore to get me some black draught. And while Mr. Mangum, the druggist, was wrapping it up he asked me had I heard the news in town that morning about young Neill Arch. I said I hadn't. Then he leant over the counter and looked around him and spoke kind of secretlike to me and said, 'Why, old Colonel MacNeill's boy, Neill Arch, was cut to death last night. Come here, let me show you.' You know he's a kind of frank-speaking man and he took me to the door and pointed out some damp sawdust blobs here and there on the sidewalk and leading around the corner. 'There's his very blood there under that sawdust,' he said. 'I sprinkled it to cover it. Uhm. I wouldn't tell everybody about it but I'll tell you.'

" 'Who in the world done it?' I asked.

" 'Ah, that's a mystery to some folks maybe but not to me,' " he said. 'And I don't mind telling you who I think done it. You know Joe McFayden, don't you?' I told him I did. 'He's a traveling salesman goes around a lot. His wife lives here in town. You know her.' 'I've seen her,' I said. And I remembered her and some of the stories I'd heard about her. Have you ever seen her?"

"I don't think so, Mr. Mac," I said.

"If you had you'd remember her. A pretty thing and built the way men like and knows it. So according to what I gathered from Mr. Mangum she had been making up to young Neill Arch in her husband's absence. And maybe that's where the box of candy come in. Young Neill Arch had bought it for her as perhaps he had bought her many another trinket. You know how women are about trinkets."

"I've not had much experience in that sort of thing," I said.

"You don't have to have experience," he retorted, "young or not young. You kind of know that to start with. The Bible's full of it. Any book is full of it. Any neighborhood you might live in shows it, shows how women are seduced and carried away by little trinkets, gifts and doodads handed out from the fingers of men. So it happened that Joe McFayden, according to Mr. Mangum, came home two nights ago and found young Neill Arch with his wife in what they call a compromising position in bed, and so he out with his knife and slashed the young man to the quick. He got away, Neill Arch did, and staggered home to his father's house to die. The blood drops led all along the sidewalk showing the path he traveled, forward but never to travel back. He made it to the drugstore and tried to get help but couldn't for it was deep in the night and the store was closed.

"Mr. Mangum seemed mighty sad and cut up about it. 'Ah,' he said to me, 'There's many things happened in this town, Mac. I've been a druggist here twenty years and I ought to know.' And he does know, for he's told me lots of things you and I like, the kind of things most people like for that matter. You know that's an interesting thing about people, they all enjoy stories. Whether they're sad or funny, they enjoy 'em just so there's a tale in 'em. And most people have got sense about how tales ought to be told. They can understand all right when a story's mishandled—whether the main point is brought out right or not. Did you know Neill Arch?"

"I used to see him some," I replied. "A fine-looking young man."

"That's what Josie Belle McFayden thought all right," and Mr. Mac let out one of his grim little chuckles.

"And now what will happen to her and her husband—if it was murder?"

"Nothing will happen to her. It will all be hushed up and things will go on as before. People know about it and they'll talk about it among themselves. But it won't come out in the open and get into the papers. And the main reason is maybe because of old Colonel Neill Arch himself. He will keep it hushed up. Right after Mr. Mangum had talked to me about it I left the drugstore and started over to buy me a strip of meat at the market and I met old Colonel Neill himself. You know what a grand looking figure of a man he is."

"Yes, I do."

"Thick drooping mustache, flower in his buttonhole, vest and gold chain and long-tailed coat. And the tobacco yes, his tobacco. He was chewing it just as usual and his mustache was all stained with it. For forty years I've heard him make his roaring speeches there in the courthouse in the cause of navigation on the Cape Fear, North Carolina's charge at Gettysburg, and how he himself fought the full three hot July days on nothing but a canteen of buttermilk, and about better schools and graded roads. In fact his life has mainly been one of talk and running for congress, and he was too young to fight in the Civil War. And he'll never be elected to congress and he'll die old and discouraged, no doubt. But people respect him, and he's got influence. He always puts on a good front just as he did yesterday morning. He stopped me on the sidewalk, held up his hand all breezy like. 'Morning, Mac,' he said to me. 'Morning, Colonel,' I said. 'I'm coming over to get some of that fine waterground meal,' he said. 'I'll bring you a peck next time I come to town, Colonel,' I said. 'That's a man,' he said, 'and how's politics on Little River?' 'About the same.' 'Guess you heard about the sorrow that's come to me.' 'Yes, it's bad, Colonel.' 'Yes, too bad,' he said. 'My boy Neill Arch died this morning, Mac. Died of galloping pneumonia. Yes, galloping pneumonia carried him off.' And he looked me straight in the face with his bright blue eyes with never a trace of a lie in 'em, all clear and innocent as a girl's.

"'I'm sorry,' I mumbled, 'real sorry, Colonel.'

"'But as the Lord says in his blessed book,' he said, 'death took him in the night like a thief that falls upon his victim unawares.' And his voice took on a loud note just as if he was getting ready to make a speech. Then he caught himself and said all quietlike, 'Poor little Neill Arch.' And with that he pulled out his big stained handkerchief, blew his nose, and wiped away his tears. He smoothed back his mustache, fixed the flower in his buttonhole, and tipped his hat. 'You are my friend,' he said. 'Come to the funeral, Mac.' 'Goodbye, Colonel,' I said, and he went on down the sidewalk, his heavy stomach stuck out in front of him all proud and stifflike as if he had just been nominated for congress and not shaded and shamed down to death. So there won't be anything said about the murder. They are burying young Neill Arch there in Tirzah graveyard with his ancestors, the proud dead Scotsmen of old. And all will be hushed up finally and things will go on just the same with the turning world, the rising and the setting sun and the stars up high looking down on it all like they've looked for millions of years and like they will look for millions more. And it's right that it is so. It's right, Paul."

"Maybe so, Mr. Mac. Yes," I said.

WASHING CLOTHES

From *The Frank C. Brown Collection of North Carolina Folklore*, Vol. I, Duke University Press, 1952. Reprinted by permission of the artist, Clare Leighton.

A Note on the Author

Paul Green, playwright, novelist, essayist, and short story writer, was born near Lillington, North Carolina, in 1894. He received his early education at Buies Creek Academy in Harnett County in the Cape Fear Valley. After receiving a degree from The University of North Carolina at Chapel Hill and pursuing graduate study at Cornell, he became professor of philosophy at the University in Chapel Hill, and later taught graduate courses in creative writing there. He has been awarded honorary degrees by The University of North Carolina at Chapel Hill and a number of other universities and colleges. He was twice given Guggenheim fellowships for study of the theatre in Europe and in 1951 was lecturer in many Asiatic countries for the Rockefeller Foundation. He was a member of the executive committee of the United States National Commission for UNESCO and served as delegate to the UNESCO conference at Paris. He has been a member of the National Institute of Arts and Letters since 1941.

In 1927 he received the Pulitzer Prize for the best American play of the year, *In Abraham's Bosom*, and he is author or co-author of numerous motion picture scripts. His list of published works follows:

The Lord's Will and Other Plays, 1925
Lonesome Road (six plays for the Negro Theater), 1926
In Abraham's Bosom and the Field God, 1927

In the Valley and Other Plays, 1928
Wide Fields (short stories), 1928
Tread the Green Grass (a folk fantasy), 1929
The House of Connelly and Other Plays, 1931
The Laughing Pioneer (novel), 1932
Roll Sweet Chariot (play), 1934
Shroud My Body Down (play), 1935
This Body the Earth (novel), 1935
Hymn to the Rising Sun (play), 1935
Johnny Johnson (play), 1936
The Lost Colony (play), 1937
Out of the South (fifteen selected plays revised), 1939
The Enchanted Maze (play), 1939
The Highland Call (play), 1939
The Hawthorn Tree (essays and letters), 1943
Forever Growing (a credo for teachers), 1945
Salvation on a String (twenty-one short stories), 1946
The Common Glory (play), 1948
Dog on the Sun (stories), 1949
Faith of Our Fathers (play), 1950
The Common Glory Song Book, 1951
Peer Gynt (modern adaptation of Ibsen's play), 1951
Dramatic Heritage (essays), 1953
Wilderness Road (play), 1955
The Founders (play), 1956
The Confederacy (play), 1958
Drama and the Weather (essays), 1959
Wings for to Fly (three radio plays), 1959
The Stephen Foster Story (play), 1959
Plough and Furrow (essays), 1963
Five Plays, 1963
Cross and Sword (play), 1964
The Sheltering Plaid (play), 1965
Texas (play), 1966
Texas Songbook, 1967
Words and Ways, 1968

3 1801 00029 7782